Sky Fleet of Atlantis

The Darkworld Legends

Dragon Paths
Sky Fleet of Atlantis

Frena Bloomfield

Sky Fleet
of Atlantis

**EEL
PIE**

© Frena Bloomfield 1979
First published 1979 by Eel Pie Publishing Ltd.,
5 Langley St, Covent Garden, London WC2H 9JA

ISBN's
Hardback edition: 0 906008 05 0
Paperback edition: 0 906008 07 7

Set in Times Roman by Computacomp (UK) Ltd., Fort William, Scotland,
and printed and bound in Great Britain by
William Clowes (Beccles) Limited, Beccles and London

1

SHE screamed when they told her. They drew back from her and the priests tried to comfort her, but she refused to let them calm her.

'We've waited so long for him,' she wept, 'and now you'll take him from us.'

'No, no,' they said soothingly, but in a way she was right and they knew it. Her husband stood beside her, looking strained and unhappy. She turned on him too.

'You could stop them!' she cried.

'It is written,' he said helplessly. 'How can we argue with the Seers?'

She turned from him contemptuously and the White Company watched her almost admiringly. She was like a tigress defending her cub. She cared nothing for any of them.

'I haven't waited all these years to lose my only child to your schemes,' she raged at them.

They were silent. Her words shocked them, although they realised she spoke so wildly only because of her grief.

'He will be yours for a time,' said the High Priest gently. 'You shall have him for his childhood, but after that you mustn't grudge him to us. He'll save us all—all Atlantis, and all the children not yet born. Can't you see that? Can you only see your own wishes?'

She understood the rebuke and grew calmer. They breathed a sigh of relief. Their only hope of survival—as the one source of light within all that darkness—was in holding together. If anyone broke away from them—and now of all times—they would be lost.

'Take him,' said the same priest as he put the newborn babe back into his mother's arms. 'Take him and cherish him.'

The child cried, the strong wailing cry of a baby distressed at being thrown out into the rough world from the cradle of the womb. She hugged him to her, whispering against his soft cheek.

She put it out of her mind, as far as that was possible among the ugliness and the shadows surrounding them. It was almost possible.

Her husband watched her carefully but eventually he too grew more philosophical. The future seemed far off and, meanwhile, there was the present. There were all the months of helping a small boy to take his first steps. The years of answering questions. The seasons coming and going, while the boy grew up through them all. And, despite everything, there was some light.

The work went on too, for that was sacred. Her husband attended to that, for she had her other duties now. It was he who spoke for them at the ceremonies. It was he who renewed the oaths for them. It was he who now held their place in the secret company. Eventually it was he who was made a priest, in honour of his position as the father of that long-awaited child.

As far as the world was concerned, he was just another merchant, successful and absorbed in making money. His child would fall heir to his small trading empire. Among his friends were many Templars. Ordinary people went in fear of him because of his associates. He was a man above suspicion.

'Incredible that no one has ever marked us down,' murmured the Elder of the priests.

'Not so strange. This is a land of many secrets.'

'True enough, but this light has been burning for long years now—and no reflection cast from it!'

'Not for much longer, surely?'

'We can only hope not. We can only hope.'

He was alone in the darkness they had raised about him. A small boy afraid of the night. He stood rooted in the circle. They had warned him not to move. They said: in the circle you will be safe. They said: remember what we have taught you. Then they had drawn the darkness down about him.

He was ten.

He waited. For a long time. Time passes very slowly for a young boy. A boy afraid. There was a sound, out in the night. He strained to hear it. He could see nothing. Only the circle glowing dimly around him.

There was a muttering—out there. He moved uneasily. He was standing on his own name, written clear within the circle. Next to it the name of his father and mother.

A shriek rose out of the darkness. A single rending scream as if a human being was torn apart. Silence. Then a succession of dreadful cries. Above it, rising wave upon wave now, the howling came. The shrieking of fiends throwing themselves into hideous paroxyms of rage. The darkness writhed with monsters.

The convulsing shadows and the noise came down about him. Lightning exploded in his face, blinding him. They were gathering around him. They were hungry. Seeking for a way to reach him. To break him.

He touched the prayer-roll strapped to his forehead. They gathered closer. He could feel them, see them, hear them—threatening and demanding. Their evil came in wave on wave against him.

They took other forms, their shapes shifting even as he tried to see them. Beasts with hooked claws and snarling teeth, slashing at him, trying to rend him with those hooks.

He closed his eyes, repeating to himself the sacred words that tamed them. All the while he had to fight down his own fear. If his spirit failed him, these creatures would mark him. They would bring darkness into his own soul. They said: if the darkness once comes into you, you will never know peace. If he could not take these beings, he would lose everything. His lips moved. His eyes stayed tightly shut.

As he went resolutely through the words of control, his confidence gradually mounted. They were answering, these dark guardians of the outer gates. Bowing to the ritual. It was true what they had told him. They said: the words are the symbol of power and even a child well-taught could use them.

Their shapes changed yet again. Gradually they came near to being human. At first, they were men of wild aspect. Savages. Then, more slowly now, their faces grew calm and they were more still. They crowded closely to the edges of the circle, calling gently to him.

'Child, come out!'

'We will not harm you.'

'Let us come and pay respect to you. See, we have submitted.'

They beckoned to him, but he would not acknowledge them. He had learned the long lessons well. They said: never open the circle until the spirits have been banished whence they came. They were silent now. He looked steadily from face to face. They were smiling, but their smiles were awry. Evil.

Then—it came. Slithering in the darkness beyond the men or manshapes standing there. Sliding towards him leaving a trail of slime. Its shapeless body oozing round the circle, spilling out as if the substance of its flesh would give way and let the carcase spill out across the floor.

A rank stench of corruption and decay arose from it, as if it had feasted for years on corpses. The boy shuddered.

They began to call to him again out of that night. One voice, then another. One before, one at the side. As they called from one direction and he turned to the sound, another voice drew him round again. A chorus rose all about him. He stared around him wildly, losing that precious concentration. The slimy thing crept closer, stinking matter drowning his senses in confusion.

Everything together—noise, stench, fevered movement, that crawling beast. He was beleaguered by them all. But, though he trembled, though his flesh prickled with revulsion, he would make no move to retreat. He held grimly to everything they taught him.

Then—cutting like silver ice through all those things of darkness came a sound. High, thin, pure. The silver flute of the Servant of Light. With a note so perfect that those distorted beings fled away before its judgment. Back into their home of night, while the boy saw dawn rising all about him. Light overriding dark.

They said: there is no darkness, only the shadows of your heart. Death will fade into life, dark into light. Then they came to him with arms outstretched, smiling, and he took their welcome gravely for he somehow knew that this company had marked him out and set him apart—just as they themselves were set apart on this dark continent.

He nodded and they sensed that he had aged. Some of them were sorry at this dark maturing of such a young boy, but it was inevitable. They gathered round him and grew silent as the Priest Magician prepared the sacrament.

In his right hand he held a diamond on a golden chain. The stone was tiny but it cast a radiance of its own. Gently he placed it round the boy's neck.

'Take this as a remembrance of that other stone, lost beneath the snows, for the virtue of this small gem is nothing beside the purity of that lost stone.'

The boy touched it with his own right hand. In spite of its cold light, it felt strangely warm to the touch as if some inner fire were contained in it.

Then the Priest Magician took a little phial of oil. He dabbed it on the boy's eyes, mouth and hand. It left a slight burning feeling wherever it touched.

'With this oil I seal the three betrayers—*eyes, mouth, hand*—that you will never reveal any knowledge of the White Company to those outside our fellowship.'

Then he took the Emblem of Light from the High Master's hand and touched the boy's shoulders with it. The boy jerked as if an electric shock had jarred his nerves.

'With this Emblem—the symbol of our sacred knowledge—I give protection to you, so that no man outside the White Company shall see into your heart.'

They were close about him now, their eyes upon him.

The Priest Magician continued.

'Because you have survived the ordeal by terror, we honour you. Because you have trusted our teaching and used it well, we will share our strength with you, knowing that you will safeguard those teachings. Because you are he whom we await, we kneel to you.'

There was just the rustle of robes as they all knelt before him, heads bowed. He stood gazing down at them. Then they rose and embraced the boy warmly.

'Remember,' said the Priest Magician with his arm about the boy's shoulder, 'Whatever the terrors of this dark land, the White Company stands with you. Even beyond death, we shall come to you if you need us. Just as you will come to us when we need you.'

Then he took the oath before them.

*   *   *

The great hall was filled only with the hiss of cloth flowing to the floor and touching it as they walked. They came in two lines, hooded and robed. Faces concealed within the shadows of their hoods, so that they looked faceless and somehow more menacing. Flickering torches were fixed in brackets all along the walls, seeming to emphasise the darkness. They went to their bench and seated themselves, elbows on the long table. Twelve of them. Throwing back the hoods, pale faces and cold eyes revealed themselves. The Tribunal of the Templars.

He stood before the Tribunal of the Templars and his father stood beside him. He was fourteen. The twelve stared at him, their piercing eyes trying to get down inside him if they could. He looked back at them calmly, allowing no careless thought to shadow his mind. If they found it there they would tear the truth from him.

The questions came and the answers were made by him. He did it well. His father watched and listened. The boy was only fourteen—yes—but he was a man in guile. In a land of treachery, he was a master among them all. The truth was hidden so deep in him that not even the Tribunal of Templars could find it. He faced them proudly, with just the right amount of uncertainty that would make them feel him to be true.

It was successful. The test over, they welcomed him into their company and so opened the way to their own downfall.

The Master of the Templars appointed him to be a body servant. It was thought to be an honour, but in reality he was little more than running boy for the whims of the Master. If the Master was sleepless, he had to spend the night reading to him even, though his own eyes might be drooping with fatigue. If the Master was angry, he was literally a whipping boy and many a night he crawled to bed groaning from the pain of a beating.

He was only fourteen. Just a boy. But he watched and learned and took note of everything without anyone paying him much attention. Even the Master often forgot the silent boy in his presence. Evil gathered about him but it could not touch him.

He would never be theirs, and they would never know that—until the time came.

2

THE great birds glided lazily over the harbour, calling harshly to each other from time to time. They were waiting for their next meal. It would be ready quite soon now, when the fishermen had finished gutting their catch. As soon as they threw the offal into the blue water of the harbour the birds would swoop. Crying triumphantly as they scooped up one greedy beakful after another until the water was clear again. That was how it had been for two thousand years.

The twins, Kerin and Pala, watched all this from above. They leaned on their elbows and watched the flight of the white birds. They said nothing. There was no need to speak. They were twins, and understood each other's moods.

'Monsterly creatures!' grunted Bron as he passed.

'Will they hurt us?' asked the girl fearfully, as the white birds brushed the tops of the sails with their wings and set the craft to shivering. Her brother laughed.

'Not they,' said Bron. 'They're just waiting on the fishermen down there.' He pointed to the surface of the ocean where the boats were huddled together. The twins looked down at the wrinkling sea, some thirty feet below their craft harnessed to the harbour wall.

'They're only harbour birds, not sea birds. Tame things!' said Bron with scorn. Suddenly he swung a blow at Kerin's ear, landing it square and making Kerin howl. Pala flinched at the pain which echoed in her own mind.

'Filthy little animal! If I catch you doing that again I'll take a rope-end to your backside,' he roared.

'Sorry,' muttered Kerin, who had been amusing himself by spitting on the upturned faces of the landmen below.

'We're tired of being watched all the time,' said Pala plaintively. 'Ever since we came here they've been staring at us— as if we were strange beasts in a cage.'

'It's seldom enough they have a chance to see the Sky Fleet anchored. Don't begrudge it to them.'

'What's it like to be a land-man?' asked Kerin.

'It's so long since I've been there I've almost forgotten,' said Bron. 'Let me think a moment.'

Bron was unusual in that he was one of the few sky-people to have been born on the land. Most were born into the Sky Fleet and lived and died as part of the fleet. Occasionally, however, the Templars would send a land-man to the Sky Fleet, or one of the fleet would be summoned to Atlantis. Bron had been one such person. At the age of eight, screaming with fear and misery, he had been dragged aboard while his parents watched gravely by that same harbour wall where the craft was harnessed now. They had stood there sadly while the ship soared up and gracefully away into that unknown element, the sky. Drifting towards the horizon it slowly disappeared from their view, and so Bron was taken from his family.

'Well,' said Bron at last. 'Imagine if you can a land where the ground is always still beneath your feet, never moving with weather. Where the sky touches down at the edge of a field, instead of being unreachable and always beckoning you further on. It's like being one of those harbour birds that have great wings and never really use them.'

'Like being tame?' asked Kerin.

'Exactly.'

A commotion in the street below drew their attention. 'Here comes the Technician,' warned Kerin.

'Let me get him aboard then.'

The twins left him to the task of lowering the ladder and made their way to their own quarters. A tiny dog ran to greet them excitedly and Pala swept him up and pressed her face into his wriggling body.

Kerin tried to distract the dog. He tugged its ears spitefully, making it yelp in protest.

'Leave him alone,' said Pala.

Kerin tugged again. The dog yelped and looked at him reproachfully.

'Go away and leave us alone!' she shouted.

'All right, I don't care. I think you're both extremely boring anyway.' Kerin sauntered away, whistling heartlessly and the dog whimpered.

Pala ran to her cabin, slammed the door shut and threw herself down on the bunk in tears. She wept bitterly, the little dog watching her in puzzlement. After a long time she stopped, exhausted and drained of feeling. She could not understand her own reaction, nor Kerin's. They were growing apart, and neither of them knew why. Kerin was irritated and Pala was miserable and both were frightened by the distances between them. Before this, they had no need of others. Now there were spaces that made in them a hunger for people, and yet could not be satisfied.

There came a knock at the door. Hastily Pala scrubbed her face to try to hide the fact that she had been crying.

'Pala?' It was her mother.

'Yes?' she answered tremulously.

'Open the door, my dear.'

Obediently she opened the door and her mother came in, seeing immediately that Pala had been weeping.

'Oh no!' she sighed. 'Not more tears! Now what's troubling you?' Mutely Pala shook her head.

'You mustn't go on like this,' said her mother more gently. 'There isn't any reason to weep so often.'

'I know.'

'Perhaps there's something wrong? Something I could help you with?'

'No.'

Her mother sighed again, more impatiently this time. Lalia was a strong straightforward woman and she found these strange moods of darkness in her daughter beyond her understanding. To her, life was simple. To eat, to drink, to sleep. To be happy when there was cause, to feel sad when bad happened. That was how she saw the world. Shifting moods and shadowy fears were quite beyond her comprehension.

'Well,' she said with determined cheerfulness, as if she hoped it might be catching, 'You must tidy yourself up. Your father wants to see you in his cabin, both of you. Go and wash your face—and try to look happier.' She gave Pala a friendly push and the girl went to the water-room to bathe her face in fresh rain-water. She paused there for a while, listening to the soothing drip-drip-drip of water seeping from the barrels and easing itself into the moist cool atmosphere. Then, looking only a little less as if she had been crying for half an hour, she made her way to her father's cabin. There, she knocked timidly and entered when he called her to do so. The cabin was an impressively large room, with a great window open to the sky. The walls were lined with shelves and charts lay on every one. These were the pathways to the secret parts of the world. From this room her father ruled the Sky Fleet of Atlantis as its master.

He was tall like her mother. But, whereas her mother was a raw-boned woman with a handsome face and an almost brawny look about her, her father was slender in face and body and had green eyes with an expression in them that spoke of the wandering horizon and the mysteries of the seas he had travelled. Her mother had the practical strength to run the food, the things of family and care for the sick, but her father had some other much less tangible kind of power. She slightly feared her mother's brusque strength but she trembled before the less defined and deeper reaching force that marked her father separate from the rest of the Sky Fleet. She was more like him than she knew at this stage and her parents both recognised it, her mother seeking to control her moods and father pitying them, knowing something of her depths from his own heart.

Her father was seated at his desk right now. Behind him sat the Technician, his pale eyes upon her. Her brother was already there, standing stiffly before the two men. He had an odd expression on his face and his eyes looked tense and strained. He smiled at her, but his eyes stared out in shock. She glanced at her father and found there the same shock, the tight sense of something unpleasant.

'My dear child,' said her father gently and suddenly she was afraid. They were not usually a tender family.

'What's wrong? What's happening?' she cried and there was a brief awkward silence. Her father coughed.

'I would not say,' put in the Technician blandly, 'that there was anything wrong. Indeed, your family has been honoured. However, you may take a little time to get used to the idea.'

'Your brother has been elected to the Company of the Templars. He is to be a land-man on Atlantis. It is a great honour,' said her father dully and his eyes said nothing.

'They're not going to take him away!'

'I know it seems hard,' her father tried to console her. 'You are twins and therefore you're closer than most brothers and sisters. But, think, there would have come a time anyway when you'd be separated. That's a normal part of life.'

'We'll never be parted.'

'Certainly you will. When you're older you'll marry and one day you'd have children of your own and they'll mean more to you than even your own twin brother does right now. In the same way, Kerin will take a wife and be closer to her than to you.'

'But I wouldn't have to leave the Sky Fleet then, would I?' Kerin put in. 'I wouldn't have to be a land-man—a tame thing!'

He looked at the Technician challengingly as he said this and the Technician flushed slightly. Kerin smiled to himself, pleased that he had struck home.

'You're being granted a great honour,' began the Technician blusteringly.

'I don't want land honours. I want to stay here and become Master of the Sky Fleet, just as my father is. I want nothing to do with the Templars.'

'It is written in the Book of Knowledge where all our futures are recorded and the Seers have read this for you. You can't argue with your fate. No man can challenge the stars to combat.'

'I can.'

Kerin's father smiled into his beard when he heard his son's brave but pointless defiance. It made the boy seem very young indeed.

The technician smiled thinly. 'That's your inexperience speaking, and we have to excuse it. You'll understand these things better as time goes on.'

'Father, you can't let Kerin go. You can't let him leave us.'

'My dear, if it's written, what can I do?'

'As you so wisely say,' observed the Technician as he rose and left the cabin.

When he closed the door quietly behind him, Pala dissolved into tears.

'I'm sorry,' said her father. He came round from behind his desk to comfort her, but she pushed him away angrily.

'You're not sorry. You don't have any feelings, any of you, and

I hate you all!' and she rushed out of the room. Her father put his hand to his forehead and rubbed it to and fro as if to remove the worry lines which creased it.

'Kerin,' he said at last very wearily, 'Go and look after your sister. Be kind to her.'

Slowly the boy went to his sister's cabin. He hesitated outside her door and then reluctantly knocked. There was silence, but he knew she was there. He could feel her there, waiting, absorbed in misery. Waves of it came out to him.

'Let me come in,' he said softly through the keyhole.

'No.'

'Open the door.'

'I won't.'

'Pala, please, we mightn't have much more time together. Don't do this while we could still be talking.'

Immediately she threw open the door and flung herself at him. Awkwardly he held her, feeling almost paternal to her in her abject unhappiness.

'You can't leave me here and go to be a land-man,' she snuffled at last, still clinging to him.

'What choice have I got? When the Templars give an order, it has to be obeyed. I'm just a boy. What can I do? We're at their mercy—all of us. You know that.'

'I hate them!' she burst out. 'What right have they got to make us unhappy?'

'You mustn't say such things. What if they found out?' He looked frightened and he held his hand over her mouth as if to trap any further outbursts before they could emerge.

At the mention of the Templars, they both felt them looming like malignant ghosts in the air about them, pressing in to listen or to watch. The twins looked about them as if they expected to see the Templars materialise in the very air surrounding them and the room trembled with their own terror. They clung together, both like small frightened children now, and then the air seemed suddenly to clear. Their sense of oppression lightened and they felt released from fear.

The small dog crept out from under the bed where he had been hiding and whined for comfort. Absently Pala picked him up and soothed him.

'Why do we have to obey them?' she whispered.

'Because we're the servants of Atlantis, I suppose. I don't know really. I never think about it.'

'I always think about it,' she said fiercely.

'Perhaps you shouldn't,' he said soberly.

'Kerin?'

'Mm?'

'Do you want to be one of them?'

'No,' he said but slowly, as if suddenly he was unsure.

She felt afraid again, as though she were already losing him.

'You couldn't want to be with them. You couldn't!'

'Oh, what's the use of thinking about it anyway. Whatever happens, I can't choose. I can't control anything. Stop asking me. I don't know. I'm not sure of anything. I don't know what I feel or what I want, and the Technician says that people often don't really know what is in their hearts—that sometimes it has to be shown to them before they really understand. He says that when I become a Templar, I'll be able to read all men's hearts, including my own.'

'Perhaps when you're a Templar, you won't have a heart for anyone to read,' she said soberly.

For answer, he shrugged.

'But we still have a little time,' she pleaded.

He smiled at her, feeling very old again. 'Yes,' he said too gently. 'We have a little time.'

They looked at each other, reflecting the same wry smile.

'Bron, when you've finished roaring like the storm clouds clashing against each other, perhaps I may continue,' Arguilo sounded stern but his eyes were twinkling.

It was the same before every voyage. An hour of obscenities from Bron when he discovered where they were going—which was never where he wanted to go.

'To the Ice Lands. It'll take a year! And the cold! Don't you remember how we all suffered last time? How all the little ones died?'

'Would I not remember?'

Too late Bron recalled that the Master's own baby had died on that sad voyage. Only a few months old, the baby had lain whimpering in his cot for days until one day he lay too quiet. The little face was blank and unresponsive and no smile answered their frantic attempts to rouse him. In that stillest of morning hours the baby died. The twins had watched horrified as their mother—that strong and unemotional woman—had wept aloud and pulled at her hair until they all had to restrain her. They were too young then to understand death properly, but grief they had learned and the fear of knowing that their parents could be broken.

'I'm sorry,' said Bron. 'I wasn't thinking.'

'It's all right. Don't worry. Look, I don't want to go to the Ice Lands any more than you, but we're the servants of the Templars. The Templars desire the Jewel from the Heart of the Ice, so we have to bring it to them.'

'What would they want such a thing for?'

'How should I know? I'm a simple navigator.'

'And we have to go to the coldest corner of the world for their errands—pah!' Bron spat on the deck and ground his spittle into the wood.

'I'm sorry to have to say this, Bron,' Arguilo leant close and spoke in lowered tones, 'but your name has been spoken to me by the Technician.' Bron paled slightly. The Technician was the eye of the Templars. Everything that happened on board was reported back to Atlantis by the Technicians, one on each vessel. From the point of view of the Sky Fleet, however, he was much more important—only he had the knowledge to power the crafts. Through his secret training, he could watch and control the flight of each craft, enabling it to sail effortlessly through the skies just above the surface of the waves.

'The Technician feels that you aren't—well, happy,' Arguilo finished weakly and Bron bit his lip. He knew that this was stern warning to watch his tongue.

'I am happy to serve you, my captain,' Bron answered formally.

'It is our task to serve the Templars, Bron.'

'Perhaps.'

'Not perhaps, Bron. It is our task. That is our duty. Not perhaps, but definitely. We are essential to the people of Atlantis. Everything that comes from other lands comes through us. Whatever the Templars need, we must bring. Whether it is the Jewel from the Heart of the Ice or the Essence of Sunset Flower—we must bring it. That is our sacred duty, Bron. We cannot question our sacred duty. Can we?'

Bron was silent.

'Can we?' said Arguilo insistently.

'Not everyone agrees with that,' said Bron at last.

'Only because you spent the whole of the last voyage persuading them so,' said Arguilo impatiently. 'Bron, I'm trying to tell you as gently as I can that you must watch your tongue. You are putting yourself in danger and I'd be very unhappy to see you come to harm. Very unhappy,' he said emphatically.

'But what I say is true, Master.'

'I don't want to hear that. You know what happened to Uran when he did the same. They cut his tongue out altogether and he was never able to use it unwisely again. You and I have been good friends for many years now and I want it to stay that way.'

Bron bent to speak into his ear. 'Don't you in your secret dreams ever want to go where you please? Don't you want to be as free as those great white fish we see from time to time, wandering the oceans as the spirit moves them?'

Arguilo stared at him, shocked and momentarily fevered. Then he answered harshly. 'The Templars can read my heart and find only loyalty in it. Now go away and ask yourself if the same is true of you.'

The fleet stirred with the excitement of departure. Down in the harbour, the land-men were running to see the fleet take wing again. Arguilo's craft would lead, the others following like ponderous geese in a stately procession. This was the moment— when the tethering ropes were released. Then the craft would set out towards the horizon and the waves might reach up hungrily to them, or the rains beat against them, but they would never falter on their steady journey.

All the Sky Fleet were out on the decks, the children leaning over the edges of the craft and waving to the land-men gaping up from the harbour wall. Down in the centre hold, the animals were crying out catching the excitement. The cows nuzzled their calves into quietness, calming them with long liquid strokes of their tongues on the little beasts sides. The hens tickered nervously and the cats washed their faces with sharp quick movements, to show they did not care.

'Look, we're going, we're going!' chanted Kerin, digging Pala in the ribs.

'It'll be the last time,' she wept and Kerin tried to console her, too full of the moment to concentrate.

'Oh just enjoy this and don't worry about anything else.'

'How can you say that!' she shouted reproachfully and ran off back to her cabin.

Kerin stared after her for a moment then shrugged his shoulders. Bron caught this and grinned at him.

'Women!' he scoffed. 'There's no understanding them. Don't even try or they'll turn you inside out with their ideas.'

Ruefully, Kerin felt this might even be true.

3

PALA lay awake deep into the night. She listened to the hundred noises of the craft in flight, her mind turning the interview with her father over and over in weariness. Kerin had gone quietly to his cabin and they had not talked about it, although both were full of questions and fears.

Suddenly she sat up. A faint sound trickled to her, disturbing her self-absorption. It was a very soft sound, almost nothing among the creakings and groanings of the craft. A murmur only, nearly lost among the sleepy grunts of the animals and the laughter of the men on night watch. A little tremor. Someone crying.

She listened intently. It continued. It was not Kerin—that she knew because she would have felt his crying before there was any sound to it. The young children were all safely with their mothers who would never have let them weep so hopelessly in the darkness. No one was ill, as far as she knew. Yet someone was certainly very unhappy.

It was very dark in her cabin. Outside there was still a faint glow in the sky—the last of the sunset lingering over the rim of the world. And the stars were bright, but there were shadows gathered in her cabin and she was afraid of them. All the Sky Fleet feared the night. It was whispered that strange and ugly things happened under darkness. They were all the children of sunlight and day.

However, that continuing cry of sadness roused her and she swung her feet over the edge of the bed and, pulling her robe protectively about her, she made her way to the door.

Outside she could hear the voices of the watchmen more clearly, and that too gave her courage. Out in the dark corridor she stood quite still and listened carefully, trying to locate the sobbing.

'Pala!'

She gasped in fright and her hand went automatically to her throat. Kerin was standing behind her, bare-footed and in his nightshirt.

'What are you doing out here?' he demanded. 'I knew you were frightened so I came.'

'Can't you hear it?' she said.

'What?'

'Ssshh, listen.'

He did. Both of them could now quite clearly hear that unrelenting weeping.

'Who is it?' he whispered.

'I don't know, but I think we ought to go and see.'

Hand in hand they walked up the narrow passageway, tracing the noise back to its source—not a very difficult task as they drew closer. They came to a halt outside a door. From there they heard it plainly. Quiet, distinct and forlorn.

'Let's go in then,' she said.

But they hesitated, embarrassed and also reluctant to intrude on that private sorrow. Then they caught each other's eye and giggled suddenly without really knowing why.

'Do you think I'd better go in?' asked Kerin and she nodded.

He opened the door cautiously and they peered into the cabin. There was a light—just a flickering candle, but enough to see by. Someone was lying on the narrow bed, face down upon the pillow, head buried in his arms.

Whoever it was seemed completely unaware that they were there. They stared at the occupant of the bed and then looked at each other. Pala bit her lip uncertainly, then she mouthed 'You speak to him' to Kerin. Her shook his head and whispered 'No, you do it'. As if by instinct the stranger looked round at them and gazed through swollen eyes at the intruders.

'What do you want?' he said in a muffled voice, through which they could plainly hear his resentment.

'We didn't mean …'

'Get out of here,' he said fiercely.

'Well, I …'

'Get out!'

'No!' said Pala boldly, surprising even herself. 'We want to know who you are and why you're making all this noise. You can be heard all over the ship, you know.'

'If it were me,' put in Kerin, 'I'd be ashamed of myself.'

Pala dug him in the ribs indignantly.

'I didn't realise,' said the stranger in deflated tones. 'I didn't mean to.'

'Who are you?'

'My name is Larn.'

'That's a land name,' said Kerin.

'Well, I'm a land-man.'

'Then why are you here.'

'Because … because …' to their discomfort he dissolved into tears again and his words were swallowed up in sobs.

'Perhaps we shouldn't have come, after all,' whispered Pala. 'It's not really our business, is it?'

'No, I want to find out what he's doing here. Let me go and talk to him.'

So saying, Kerin went over and grabbed hold of the stranger's arm and shook him fiercely. He spoke to him in a hard voice, no pity in it.

'Come on, stop crying. We sky-farers stop blubbing when we're five years old. Don't tell me men are like children back on land!'

Larn grew angry. He shook off Kerin's hold and spat back at him: 'If you were me, you'd have enough to cry about till you were fifty. But I'll only weep tonight. Never again. No matter what happens.'

He stared them down and then seemed to notice for the first time that they were twins. He looked from one to the other, marvelling at their likeness.

'What are your names?' he asked at last, in a normal voice.

'I'm Kerin and this is my sister Pala.'

'I see.'

'Now will you tell us what you're doing here?'

'All right. I suppose you'd better sit down. Here, take this so you won't get too cold.'

He tossed a thick robe over and they wrapped it round themselves and sat down by the narrow bed. Larn looked at them. His face, when it was not swollen with crying, seemed a pleasant one. Not handsome, certainly, but open and friendly with a large mouth that emphasised his smile on its rare appearances.

'Well?' Kerin prompted him.

'My parents died in a fire. Our house burned down.'

'But you were saved?'

'I was out at a friend's house for the night and it happened while I was away. When I got back home next day, there was nothing left. Just black ruins and some smoke rising from the charred wood.'

'What a terrible accident,' said Pala, tears of sympathy already standing in her eyes.

'It wasn't an accident. It was done deliberately.'

Both the twins looked shocked, while Larn seemed to be surprised at their reaction.

'Why yes. It's nothing so unusual, is it? Such things happen every day in Atlantis. My father was going to lay an accusation in the Temple against a corrupt Templar. That's why he was killed. That's why I'm here. My family decided I'd be safer here with the Sky Fleet so they bribed another Templar to move me here. But I can't help wanting to be back there—and wanting to see my parents again. I can't help it!'

As he seemed to be on the verge of tears again, they hastily interrupted him.

'Such things have never happened here,' said Pala.

Larn laughed bitterly.

'Well, they always say the Sky Fleet is different but it can't be that different. They say you're peaceful folk, right enough, but you must have troubles here. Power struggles and politicians, all after the leadership. Stealing and killing—you get it everywhere.'

'Not here,' said Kerin firmly. 'I've never heard of such things being done. Life isn't perfect, I suppose. We argue and we get unhappy. Maybe we want things we can't have. But not killing.'

'But there must be. And plotting, and buying power and selling favours—all those things are normal. You must have them here.'

'We don't,' said Pala. 'Our father is Master of the Sky Fleet, so we'd know, wouldn't we?'

'I wish I could believe you,' he sighed.

'But it's true!' they both shouted in unison, exasperated by him.

There came a sharp knock at the door and then it opened and Bron peered in frowning.

'Ah,' he said. 'I thought I heard something going on in here. What are you two doing here at this time of the night?'

'We just ...'

'I heard ...'

They both stopped and a nervous giggle caught their throats.

Larn watched with interest. 'Are you going to flog them?' he asked.

Bron looked at him and said sourly: 'You're not on the land now and that isn't how we sky-people live.'

'Bron, don't be cross, you old whale,' Pala pleaded softly, winding her arm through his. Bron frowned all the more fiercely to hide the twinkle in his eyes.

'Larn has been telling us such terrible things.'

'What things?' he said sharply.

'About my people—and how it is on the land.'

'Ah, yes.'

Bron understood. He carried his own memories of Atlantis and had secrets in his heart which he would keep until the time came for all secrets to be told.

'You'll find life better here, my boy,' he said quietly to Larn. 'I know how you feel right now—lost and homesick, in spite of everything back there—but you'll find peace here among the sky-farers and you'll forget the terrors of Atlantis. Believe me, I know all about that.'

He had spoken more strongly than he intended and when he realised that they were all staring at him he became embarrassed. Noisily he cleared his throat.

'Now you've got five minutes to get back to your own beds.'

'Yes, Bron,' said Kerin and immediately the door closed they fell to talking again.

'Larn, is it really like that in Atlantis?'

'Of course, how could you doubt it? What's so strange about what I've told you anyway?'

Larn shrugged. It was all beyond him to judge. He only knew what he knew and that was all. Silently the door opened again but this time it was the Technician who came in and looked at them without speaking for several moments.

'I think you should return to your cabins,' he observed at last and smiled a chill little smile.

'Yes, sir,' said Kerin obeying instantly and pulling Pala up with him. They briefly said good night to Larn.

The Technician let them go, his eyes never leaving Larn's face. Larn looked down at his blanket, feeling small and afraid under those cold eyes as if he were again in the presence of the Templars. Technician spoke and his voice was surprisingly mild.

'You'll find life easier here.'

Larn said nothing.

'It might be strange at first, but it's easier. You should be careful what you say. They are much more innocent, the sky-people. You must remember that. Life has to be different in Atlantis for reasons which you're too young to understand and you shouldn't speak too much of the past if you wish to leave it all behind as you should. I'll have to report on your progress to the Templars. I'd like to speak well of you.'

With that hint of a threat he left Larn.

Bron and Arguilo glared angrily at each other.

'There's nothing I can do, Bron, and that's all there is to it.' He started to turn away but Bron caught hold of him.

'Captain ...'

'Forget the 'captain' part, Bron. We've been together too long to need that and we know each other too well.'

'Aye, ever since that first night I was brought here, snivelling and whimpering like a lost puppy.'

'Besides which, this isn't an official discussion. In fact, as far as I'm concerned, it never happened and I shall forget all about it.'

'That's just what you mustn't do. I'm telling you, you can't allow your son to become a Templar.'

'It's a position of honour,' answered Arguilo tonelessly.

'You know better than that. The Atlantis the sky-people serve is a land of dreams. It doesn't exist. You and I both know that the real Atlantis is a land where people are afraid. Do you really intend to send your son to become part of that terror? Do you want him corrupted too?'

Arguilo shook his head and groaned: 'What can I do? It's finished now. It's their decision, not mine.'

Bron said nothing, just stared at him.

'Well,' he said exasperated, 'What do you expect me to do to fight the power of the Templars?'

'If that were a serious question,' said Bron softly, leaning forward so that Arguilo could hear him properly, 'I might have a serious answer.'

Arguilo glanced at him and then looked swiftly away, deep in thought for a moment. Then he headed towards the deck and beckoned Bron to follow him. On deck, they gazed out over the side of the craft at the distant swing of the blue ocean and the clear watercolour sky. Below the sea murmured and the sails billowed taut and full in the wind. The crew hurried about in the sunshine, glad to be journeying again. They greeted Arguilo respectfully when he came on deck and the twins waved to him. They were busy feeding the animals which was part of their daily tasks. The animals were all kept in the centre hold. A cow and her two shaky children with velvety coats and huge wondering eyes. Some scatterbrained chickens and a few smug cats to keep the mice under control.

Arguilo looked back at the rest of the fleet, drifting in the same slow yet unhesitating flight. A huge and gentle fleet. He sighed. Bron caught the sigh and said, 'You see, you're not happy about it all, are you?' As he spoke, his fingers touched the jewel at his throat in an automatic gesture.

'Even if that were true, what do you think I can do? The Technician ...'

'Exactly,' interrupted Bron. 'The Technician. He's the one we have to take care of. Oh, you're the captain. You plan our voyage. You keep the sky-people happy. You are the Master of the fleet, but he is the eye of the Templars—a spy.'

'And so?'

'Why must he be here?'

'Because he holds the secret of powering the craft.'

'That's right, and the same for every other craft in the Sky Fleet. Well, supposing we held the secret of that power too? Then there'd be no excuse for the Technician to be here.'

'That may be true, but what's the point of such talk?'

'Captain, I know his secret!'

'You? But how?'

'He's coming!' Bron warned urgently, but Arguilo had already felt the chill of the Technician's approach.

'This is a fine morning, captain.'

'It is indeed!'

'I'll do as you say, captain,' Bron saluted clumsily and went away, watched by them both.

'You find him ... co-operative?'

'Yes. I spoke with him yesterday, as you suggested. He'll be more careful now. He means no harm. He's a simple man, like a child. He blunders about like an ox, but he's well-meaning.'

'I wish I could agree,' said the Technician with menace.

He had been assigned to the Master ship for many years—as many as Arguilo had been its Master—but there was no closeness between the two men, only a cold alliance which did not include friendship on either side.

The Technician had remained apart from them all. His skin did not even bronze under the gaze of the sun as theirs did. Even the babies were brown and healthy, while he was as cold and pale as a Templar.

'Have you spoken to the boy Larn?'

'Not yet. When I've had time to finish the morning duties, I'll see him then and speak with him.'

'It would be as well to warn him that he shouldn't talk too much of the past. That's ended. He has a new life to live now.'

'He'll need time to forget.'

'He must forget now.'

'We'll help him as much as we can, but obviously he'll grieve for a while yet.'

'I've spoken to him once, but if it's necessary I'll do it again.' He walked away and the sailors watched him covertly, their eyes sliding after him.

If his shadow fell on them or his cold glance passed over them, they looked away uneasily. After he had gone, they talked too loudly and laughed too confidently, to show their carelessness.

When he saw the Technician depart, Bron came up again.

'Well?' he demanded.

'Well what?'

'You know what. Are you interested in what I have to tell you? If not, I'll keep it to myself.'

'What do you expect me to do with this knowledge?'

'Use it!'

'But how?'

'Go where we will. Trade as we wish. I'm not saying we shouldn't serve Atlantis. Of course we should, but we do it for our own price. We should be free, be our own men and follow that great white fish. Get rid of the Technician too.'

Arguilo had gone pale beneath his bronze skin.

'Lower your voice, man!' he hissed. 'You're talking mutiny!'

'Yes, I am.'

'Let me think for a while.'

'Fine enough!'

Bron went off quite cheerfully, leaving a worried man behind him. Bron could carry secrets easily—he had always borne secrets—whereas Arguilo was weighed down by them. He did not know Bron's secrets, or he might have taken heart. But his thoughts were that Bron would not be changed by the future. He would carry on as usual, irritable, grumbling and faithful to the limit of his life. Arguilo however, had to carry the whole fleet through any danger that was to come.

He shivered as strange shadows passed across the sun.

4

'You fools! What am I to tell the True Lord of Atlantis?'

The Master of the Templars glared angrily about him. His eyes passed from one bowed head to another through the assembly of Templars. They made no reply, but a murmur of uneasiness went among them. At last, Taula—long the favourite of the Master of the Templars—raised his head.

'Master, you can only tell him what is true. We have no excuse to make. We have slept while our enemies plotted against us. The blame is ours and we bow to your wrath.'

He scowled at them, but in truth the Master knew it was no use raging at them. However much the fault might lie with them, it was he alone who would have to bear the blame for this disaster.

The Templars knelt humbly and the Master left them. He made his way to the dark and fearful chamber of the True Lord of Atlantis.

'My True Lord, I pray you will pardon this intrusion into your chamber,' he began.

The room was heavy with shadows. It had huge windows, but they were firmly closed and heavy draperies shut out all trace of daylight. There was a couch in the centre of the chamber and on it lay a still figure. As the Master entered the chamber, he felt rather than saw the figure turn its face towards him.

'What is it? Why do you disturb me so?' The voice was soft and hissing, like the icy wind through the frosted leaves of autumn.

'My True Lord, I have terrible news for you.'

'Speak,' he sighed.

'The Sky Fleet has mutinied.'

The Master bowed his head now against the anger which would follow.

'Mutinied?'

Now that he had started, the Master hurried on with his news before that prone figure could speak again.

'Some are loyal to us yet,' he went on, 'Perhaps more than half the fleet. We can't tell yet, but we're trying to find out from the Technicians. We can only assume that those we don't hear from have been imprisoned by their captains. The fleet has divided. We don't know how it's happened.'

'I have the world to watch. Can I not even trust you to watch the sparrows tumble from the sky?'

'This is all my fault. I have failed you, my True Lord.'

'Who is responsible for this mutiny?'

'We don't know yet. There's too much confusion. If you would turn your mind upon the task, we would soon know all there is to know.'

'I suppose then that I must,' said the reclining figure wearily. 'Kneel beside me then and be silent.'

He was called the True Lord of Atlantis to distinguish him from that other one—the first Lord of Atlantis. He had been a weakling, a fool—so said the True Lord of Atlantis when he spoke with the Templars. He had mocked him. What a simpleton he was, he whispered contemptuously.

A singer of songs, a maker of poems, an idiot who nursed saplings in the gardens and tended flowers! A weak genius who led the Templars down the path of magic—the white path—and sought beauty with them.

Then HE came. The True Lord of Atlantis, as he called himself. He blazed in and overthrew that weak Lord, taking the Templars into his own paths.

Strangely, he was still unknown to the common people of Atlantis. But so had the other one been. They had passed the first one many times in the gardens of the palace. If they thought of him at all, they assumed he was a gardener.

This one—the evil one—they only caught whispers of him in their darkest dreams. Otherwise, he lay in this shadowed room, hidden from the destroying light, and worked slowly towards his secret plan—the Great Work. It was with that he obsessed them. They toiled day and night, without knowing what they reached towards. They only had his words to go on—and he had never exactly explained it to them. Insoluble mysteries have greater power to chain men down and seep into their mind. He knew that well.

Their vigil continued throughout the night. The Master grew stiff and his muscles shrieked with the pain of remaining in that one position all those hours. He did not dare to move. Meanwhile, that still figure on the couch made no move or sound. There was nothing that would tell whether he was turning the mighty power of his dark mind out to search among the sky-farers.

At last he stirred, groaning slightly.

'My True Lord?' murmured the Master.

'Do not fear,' he whispered. 'I think that this could be what I've been waiting for—the completion of the Great Work!'

'The Great Work?' he echoed.

'Yes. The crowning glory of all our efforts, brought about by innocent fools—what could be more fitting?'

The Master dragged himself to his feet, suppressing a gasp of pain as he straightened his knees.

'Go now,' ordered the True Lord. 'Return to me tonight and we shall decide uponour course of action.'

Relieved, but very puzzled, the Master hurried back to the assembly of Templars. He was exhausted and his face looked grey with fatigue. Outside where the dawn was coming up into the sky, the birds woke one by one.

He gestured towards one of the long windows where light was creeping into the hall. 'It's already daylight. Let us rest now, while we may.'

'But Master ...,' said one of them.

'Sleep as you can. We shall have many hours of hard work before us. I shall only tell you that, far from being angry with us, the True Lord of Atlantis has found cause for rejoicing.'

They looked at each other. 'How can that be so?' they murmured.

'Nevertheless, it is so,' he said firmly. 'Unknown to themselves the Sky Fleet have done the best possible thing to bring about the completion of that Great Work.'

They murmured among themselves again, awed by his words. The Great Work was all they ever talked about when they came together. From the first moment that a man became part of that élite company, that would be all his conversation. Even though he would not know the exact nature of the Great Work, all his waking thought was of it. Every hour of study, every task he undertook, all went into making the Great Work successful. Every time the Sky Fleet went on a voyage, it was bringing back some vital element for that Work.

They would perhaps have been more intrigued to know that not even the Master himself knew much more. He held only the shadow of that knowledge which apparently obsessed the True Lord of Atlantis.

'No more of this now! Sleep!' he ordered and they obediently filed out of the hall. Only the faithful Taula stayed with him.

'Master?' he plucked gently at the sleeve of the Master's gown.

'Why do you stay?' he asked gently.

'To learn, Master.'

'Ah, you have such a thirst for learning that you will drain me dry before very much longer.'

'Forgive me my presumption in asking, but what is the nature of the Great Work?'

'If I were to tell you I know about as little as you, would you believe me?'

Taula shook his head.

'Nevertheless, it is true. I know very little. I can see you don't believe me even now. Go and sleep, off with you.'

Taula went away, watched thoughtfully by the Master of the Templars. There was a strength in that insignificant clerk which always surprised him. He was all that a disciple should be— humble, obedient, hard-working—but always there was a slight hint of more. A hidden ambition that the Master half-approved but also half-feared.

A servant scurried along the corridor and ran into the Master in his hurry. Angrily the Master struck him across the cheek. 'Clumsy fool!' he snarled at the unfortunate fellow who clutched his hand to his burning cheek. 'If you don't watch where you're walking I'll have your eyes put out—then you'll have good excuse to act so blindly.'

It was no idle threat. There were beggars who owed their miserable state of blind poverty to the sudden rages of the Master of the Templars. The wretched man threw himself to his knees and the Master brushed him aside and went to the richly furnished chamber where he slept.

*   *   *

'I haven't had such a bad night in my life,' grumbled Bron. 'One nightmare after another.'

'Are you surprised?' asked Arguilo drily. 'We all have plenty to have nightmares about, after all.'

'Even so, never have I slept so ill.'

'That's curious. A number of the others have made the same complaint. Odd that so many should suddenly sleep so badly.'

'The Templars?'

'Surely. It's beginning earlier than I thought.'

'Well, dreams can't hurt us.'

'No, but sleepless nights can.'

'Perhaps it's just chance.'

'Perhaps.'

Arguilo sat there thoughtfully while Bron watched him.

'My poor friend,' Bron said sympathetically, 'This is hard for you.'

'I've always been loyal, Bron. Loyalty means honour to me. Oh, I think I'm doing what is right now, but I'm not happy about taking my people into danger.'

'You're not the only unhappy one this morning,' said Bron. 'There's the Technician too.'

Bron had already appointed himself as the official keeper of the Technician who was firmly chained in his cabin.

'How is he?'

'A very angry man.'

'I can imagine.'

'Will you speak with him?'

'Not until after the conference. Then I shall have to.'

There came a knock at the door and Larn entered. 'Sir, they're arriving now for the conference.'

'Very well,' said Arguilo, standing up. Larn made no move to go and Arguilo looked at him questioningly. However, the boy just cast an odd look in his direction and smiled weakly. Then he left the cabin and Arguilo and Bron exchanged glances.

'Bron, can you tell me what's wrong with that boy, because I certainly don't know?'

'No doubt he's confused. Who wouldn't be? He must be wondering what's going to happen.'

'So am I, Bron, so am I.'

Together, the two men walked up to the deck. As each craft drew near, a ladder of rope was lowered to the deck of the Master ship. Then each captain made his way steadily down the ladder until he was near enough to jump on the deck where two sailors steadied his landing.

Arguilo watched each one carefully, noting his responses. Some were excited and greeted him cheerfully. Others were obviously worried and cast odd glances in his direction. These greeted him uneasily as if they feared to show their usual companionship. Yet others were openly hostile and said nothing, only giving him a curt nod by way of acknowledgement. These were the ones he would somehow have to try to win, he knew.

The sailors of his own crew gathered to watch the arrivals, and he had not the heart to send them about their work as he should have done. He knew that many of them must be afraid, yet they were all completely loyal to him. Many of them had already come to him to pledge themselves personally to him, whatever might happen. One or two of them were being harassed by their wives, for women were always ready to see any threat to their own and he could not blame them. It took very little foresight to see that they were in danger, all of them.

When all the captains, twenty-five in number, were gathered in his cabin, he wasted no more time.

'My brothers, I don't have to tell you why we're here. We have much to discuss and I don't want to delay. First, I'd like to outline exactly what has happened, for those of you who may be confused.'

There was a murmur of agreement, but he could feel their

tension rising about him accusingly.

'You know we have uncovered the key to driving the craft. With this in our grasp, we propose to become an independent fleet. We want to control our destiny more closely than has been possible up to now.'

'What is this key you speak of?' asked Balio.

'Bron, you explain.'

Bron rose. 'It's so simple I hardly dare to stand here pretending to be any kind of authority on this. However, these are the details. The whole secret of powering these craft depends upon the interaction of water and certain crystals which are in the possession of each Technician.

'You all know we can only travel over water. Either the ocean itself or a river, stream, or even a lake or marshy ground. The crystals seem to form a force field when they react with water vapour. The more water, the greater the force. That explains why we can travel so swiftly over the ocean and so slowly over some small inland river.'

'Why does this work?'

'That I don't know. I can only know that it does. Each of you will find these crystals in the possession of your own Technicians, and I assume they will power the craft indefinitely.'

'Arguilo, you're putting us all into danger for your own gains!'

This was Marrad, a longtime rival of Arguilo's. Once it was thought that he might have been the Master of the Sky Fleet, but the position had fallen to Arguilo and he had never really forgiven this. He felt that he had lost his chance through the unjust pressure of superstition. His grandfather, a fit and healthy man until his early thirties, had died a demented cripple. So too did his father. The Sky Fleet had felt that this was something passed in his bloodline and that he also might die in the same way. Since he was robust and had never suffered any real illness in his life, he had bitterly resented this taint they cast on him. His ambition had curdled within him and soured his heart.

'This is not for my gain but for all of us,' answered Arguilo. 'You don't know what is happening on Atlantis, my friends.'

'And do you?' sneered Marrad.

'I have long known things which troubled me very much. Now that we hold the secret of our power, we can act for our own good. If we can trade on our own terms, we can do something to bring good back into Atlantis.'

'You must explain more. First, why should we wish to be independent of Atlantis? We have served her faithfully until now, so why should we wish to change that?'

'Because Atlantis has changed. Let me bring you someone who will tell you a little of what life is like there now.'

He made a signal to Bron who rose and went to the door. He returned with the boy Larn.

'Go ahead and speak,' he said kindly to the boy. 'Tell them of your life on Atlantis.'

Larn spoke to them, at first hesitantly but soon building up confidence in himself. They sat there, those honourable men, and heard him speak of the terrors of that land. Of soldiers coming to the door at night, of brothers and sisters divided against each other, of mothers betraying their own children, and all of them cowering under the shadow of the Templars.

He told them of the pain of his people and how they feared the overreaching power of the dark-minded Templars involved in their private search for knowledge. They heard him in silence. When he had finished, they still sat there without speaking a word, shocked and stunned by his words. Then Marrad spoke.

'The boy's mad!' he said. 'That's why he was sent to us—to restore his fevered brain and to clear his mind of nightmares. It's obvious!'

He made another sign and Bron again went to the door. This time there was a deathly silence as the next person entered. It was the Technician from Balio's craft.

'Captains,' he said in a voice untouched by emotion, 'you

should listen to the boy. Everything he tells you is true. There's evil—terrible unspeakable evil—in Atlantis. There's something I can't even begin to explain to you eating away at the heart of Atlantis. If you won't believe him, believe me. I'm telling you the truth. More than that, I'm prepared to stand with you in your struggle. I'll help you to the utmost of my powers, but you should take action now while you can—before the Templars have time to arm against you.'

Now they began to speak among themselves, and Arguilo let this continue without interruption, for only in that way could they come to a decision.

After several hours of talking, he raised his hand for silence.

'My brothers,' he began, 'we must make decisions regarding our future. Before you speak, let me say that I know many of you must have serious doubts. There are many dangers in what we're doing and there may be deaths too. At the moment we don't know what's ahead for us. If there are any of you who will not go with us, you must say so and go your own way.'

Then a count was taken. As the evening star grew bright in the twilight sky, he found that fifteen were with him but ten were not. Marrad spoke out for them.

'We shall be faithful to our Masters,' he said angrily. 'We'll also force you to do the same!'

Then he stood up and the nine other captains followed him out while Arguilo watched them. So it came about that the sky-people were divided.

*   *   *

There were murmurs echoing in Atlantis. Men went from one house to another, secretly, cloaked by darkness and magic against the keen eyes of the Templars.

'And is it so?' they asked of the White Magician when they were all gathered together.

'Yes,' he said.

The ceremony was made, completed, and they drew strength into their fellowship again. The Astrologer read for them while they listened keenly to him.

'When the moon makes an eclipse with the sun, then the upheavals will begin,' he said.

'And the Sky Fleet?'

'Is already dividing, as it is written.'

'They say, Astrologer, that the Sky Fleet will be destroyed. How can that be if there is to be any hope for us?'

'The Sky Fleet may take a new form—who knows? If all the future were known to us, would we have the courage to go on?' the old man said gently, his eyes staring blindly round him.

'We're living in the past, old man,' said a young man impatiently. The others hushed him angrily, but the old man smiled in the direction of the voice.

'I do not need eyes to see the obvious,' he chided. 'On the past we build our strength to help us to change the future. We've guarded our knowledge for a thousand years. If necessary we would do it for a thousand more until he comes who will use it. You're lucky—for he has come. You will see the fruition of our work.'

'Can you promise us that?' the young man bent over him, seeking to read those clouded eyes. The fellowship murmured against his lack of respect.

'No man can promise the future, haven't I just said that? I can only say that it is written.'

'Enough,' the White Magician broke in, 'we must close with the ritual against darkness. There is too much danger for us to stay here for long.'

After the ceremony, they left their meeting-place in ones and twos, so as not to draw attention. The young man walked with the Astrologer, not so much to guide him—for he had been blind since birth and knew the city well—as to talk further.

'Tell me, how do you know the truth of what is written in the stars?'

'I don't know. I only know how they should be read. Our knowledge is no longer complete. We have lost some of the keys to it.'

'Then how can you know it is still true?' he said triumphantly.

'Can a member of the White Company have such doubts?'

The young man blushed. 'I want to believe it, old man, but it's very hard. I've seen evil round me all my life. The White Company are holding to the only good in this land and they seem ...'

'... Powerless?'

'Yes—perhaps,' he mumbled.

'And is a snake not thin and powerless when it creeps through the undergrowth? But when it raises itself to strike ...'

The old man turned and in his eyes was something approaching amusement. The young man nodded, willing to be convinced.

Answering his thoughts, the Astrologer said: 'There is hope, young man.'

A small company of Templars passed them, men with dark eyes and burning minds who cast hardly more than a glance at the youth helping the old blind man to his home. Shadows moved after them, trailing them. Evil drawn to evil. An echo of something unspeakable hung behind them and they recognised it.

'That is why you mustn't lose hope. If you do that, you allow them to win.'

In the Sky Fleet the parting was not so simple. There was still the Technician. He could not be kept on board. He would be too much of a risk—an enemy so close to their heart. Arguilo spoke to him that night.

'I don't intend to apologise,' he said, 'that would seem too ridiculous. Nevertheless, I hope your stay hasn't been too unpleasant.'

'And I hope that you understand what you're doing—you and your companions,' hissed the Technician. 'And what will happen now that you refuse to send your son.'

'I've done what I must. I can't risk sending him yet. Later perhaps—yes.'

The Technician made no reply to this. He shook his head, a bitter smile on his lips. He seemed less in control than Arguilo had ever seen him before, for his hands shook with a fine tremor and his body was tense with anger during the exchange.

'We shall send you out with Marrad. I suppose he'll take you back to Atlantis, or some such arrangement.'

Arguilo was frankly embarrassed by this encounter. Always, until now, he had been deferential towards the Technician and now suddenly he really was the true Master of his ship. He felt as if he had caught the Technician at an unfair disadvantage.

However, the Technician gave no further acknowledgement of his inner disquiet. He merely nodded coolly and stood up when Arguilo had said his piece.

'And when,' he said sarcastically, 'may we expect this exchange to take place?'

'At dawn. Until then, I'm afraid we'll have to inconvenience you for one more night.'

'Tell me, Arguilo, what will you do when the whole mind of Atlantis is turned upon you? How will you withstand it?'

'I don't know, but I have confidence because I believe I'm doing right.'

'How smug you are! Since when did being right lead to victory?'

'We shall just do what we can.'

'Your own fleet will hunt you out of the skies, Arguilo. You know you'll never be safe, don't you?'

'I can't go back now. I have to trust to the future.'

'There'll be no mercy now in Atlantis for you.'

'I don't see any reason why we shouldn't be able to trade freely with the Templars.'

The Technician laughed—a chilling sound.

'You don't? My poor friend, you can't even begin to know what you're up against in this pathetic bid for freedom. No one would trade with rebellious slaves. If the wrath of Atlantis comes down upon you ...' he shook his head, not even bothering to complete the sentence.

Arguilo was uneasy. He turned to leave.

'Tomorrow,' he said, 'tomorrow at dawn we'll come for you.' He carefully barred the door again and left the Technician to his last night with the fleet. Oddly enough, although they had always been nearer to being enemies than friends, he felt almost sad that the Technician would no longer be there.

'We even miss our chains,' he muttered.

5

LARN was silent at supper. The others were too merry. They laughed and joked with a grim determination to enjoy themselves.

'As if,' thought Pala suddenly, 'as if there were no time left to them.'

She shivered and Larn looked at her. Gently he pressed his elbow against hers and she smiled. Larn was eating little and seemed to be absorbed in his own thoughts. As soon as he could, he rose from the table and left them. Kerin glanced at Larn's retreating back and then at Pala.

'I'm going after him,' she thought.

She went quietly out of the door and, if her father noticed that they had both disappeared, he gave no sign of it.

Larn was lying on his bed, staring up at the ceiling. She knocked at the door but he did not answer, so she opened the door and went inside. He still said nothing.

'What's wrong?'

'Nothing.'

'Why aren't you speaking to us?'

'I haven't anything to say.'

'Are you angry?'

'Pala, tell me, do you think your father is a fool?'

'Of course he isn't!'

'But does he really know what he's doing?'

'He's not the kind of man who makes mistakes, if that's what you mean.'

'Perhaps he's already made his mistakes.'

'What makes you think you know any better?' she challenged.

'I know what Atlantis is—and I doubt very much that your father does.'

'Don't be silly! He's the Master of the Sky Fleet. Of course he knows.'

They fell silent awkwardly. Then Pala looked up at him.

'Larn?'

'What?'

'Tell me about your life there. I want to understand! I want to *know*. I want to know what Kerin would've been doing now. If he'd gone.'

'He wouldn't have been living an ordinary life, Pala,' said Larn. 'He'd be living among the Templars. They have their own kind of life.'

'Well, tell me what *is* ordinary then.'

'It's difficult. I mean, it's hard to know where to start. Atlantis is a city, full of streets—wide streets with trees beside them—and little tiny alley-ways with houses crowded on each side. Small shops everywhere, and open markets in the squares where everyone comes to buy things.'

'Go on.' She was fascinated by his account.

'Well, outside the city, life is different again. There are green fields where the farmers keep animals and they grow crops too. They grow wheat, or maize or vegetables. Great fields of crops as far as you can see, and they're always working very hard on the land. It's good land—so they say, I wouldn't know—but it's a hard life to work it. Then around the coast there are tiny villages where fishermen live and they go out in boats, not very far, and trail nets and catch fish to bring to the city to sell. You can see the fish early in the mornings—still bright and silvery.'

'And where did you live?'

'My parents lived in a big white house set on a hill, in a very fine part of the city. There weren't any small streets near us, only big houses like ours. And trees, of course—a lot of trees everywhere around us.'

'It sounds beautiful.'

'It was, in a way, but that wasn't all there was to life. Although my parents were rich, we had some serious troubles. My father made enemies among the Templars and everywhere he went, he was followed. Many people were. You never knew who might be set to watch you. Maybe a vegetable seller in the square. Maybe your own servant. Maybe an old beggar you'd pass without a second thought. Maybe even your own best friend. My father used to warn me never to trust anyone and I suppose he was right. Everyone used to talk about it and the funny thing was that, though they all talked about it as if it didn't apply to themselves, they never treated you like a friend either. No one took any chances. I suppose you can't even imagine what it's like to feel like that. You all seem like children to me, the way you just say whatever is in your mind. It's like the little children before they learn how to be careful. That's why I wonder if even your father can know what he's doing.'

'He's a very understanding person.'

'Yes,' said Larn gently, 'but he's a stranger to Atlantis itself. All of you are. I've been here for—how long?—nearly eight days. And it really does frighten me that your father thinks Atlantis is still full of good men waiting for him to give them the chance to come up and speak out.'

Pala listened to his bitter speech, growing more angry as he continued.

'What's he supposed to do then? You're so clever—you tell me that!'

He shrugged.

'I don't know.'

'Well then!'

'In Atlantis it was sometimes said that there were groups of people who wanted to stand against the power of the Templars. We never knew any of them ourselves. We just heard whispers. But we didn't dare to show much interest in case anyone reported it.'

'But it shows there are others who think like my father.'

'Yes—and no. They knew what they were dealing with. Your father doesn't. He just wants the fleet to be independent. He doesn't really know anything about the Templars or their powers.'

'What do you want him to do then?'

'I don't know, don't ask me. I don't know!'

He shook his head, threw himself back violently on the bed and began to sob convulsively. Alarmed, Pala put her arms about his shaking shoulders and tried to soothe him.

'Don't, Larn! You mustn't. I thought you felt better now. Don't do this. Oh, I know you must miss your own home, but we'll look after you here. Please don't cry so!'

'I wanted to be safe! I wanted to sleep properly—now it's the same here. Nowhere to hide,' he gasped out between sobs. 'I thought it would be different ... they said it would ... I can't sleep at night ... dreams!'

She held him tightly and he let her wipe the tears from his face with the sleeve of her robe. She felt an immense tenderness for him.

However, he was already ashamed of his breakdown— especially before a girl—and he pushed her away from him.

'I was just being stupid,' he said angrily.

'No—I understand.'

'You understand!' he sneered. 'What do you know about it? You've been sheltered all your life. You've never suffered.'

'That isn't my fault,' she said, reasonably enough, and he suddenly had to laugh at his own self-pity.

They smiled at each other, both curious at the closeness this eruption of emotion had made between them and yet both pleased by it. Bron came in, without knocking, and sensed that he had somehow come into the middle of something which did not really involve him. However, he decided to ignore it.

'There's to be a big discussion tonight—for everyone to go to and give their opinions. Well, at least, for all those who are still with us. Your father wants you to be there as it concerns all our futures.'

'I'm tired of talking about our future,' Pala grumbled.

'You'd soon be interested if it means you being imprisoned or killed,' Bron said curtly, and reluctantly they followed him out of the cabin.

The conference was under way, but it was proceeding only slowly, for argument after argument had developed during it. At that moment, Arguilo was disagreeing with Herga, one of the captains. Kerin was watching. He was too young to speak at the conference.

'No, no, how can we go on to the Ice Lands? I haven't yet had my full instructions from the Templars.'

'But if we were still to bring back the Jewel from the Heart of the Ice, it would be a token to the Templars that we're still loyal, that we only want to be treated fairly,' said Herga earnestly.

'The trouble is,' explained Arguilo, 'that we can't return to Atlantis until we're in full contact with the Templars again. It would be too dangerous to put ourselves right back in their power until we had settled the matter first.'

'Well, Master,' put in another captain, 'then what are we to do? You persuaded us we should trade freely and we've agreed to that. Now you tell us we just have to wait until we are instructed by the Templars what we shall do. Supposing we can't live by trading, what then?'

Bron interrupted.

'We can live, friend. We can wander the whole earth and find food for ourselves.'

'Agreed, but I have no wish to live as an exile with no home. We are still part of Atlantis. We can't leave our own people and lose our roots there among them.'

'Give me time to negotiate with the Templars.'

'How?'

'The Technician will do it for us,' Targon indicated the Technician of Balio's craft. He stook up as they all looked at him.

'My friends, I will give you my name and you need no longer call me Technician. My name is Aramin.'

They murmured approval. A Technician never gave his birthname away in case his enemies used its power against him. They were known only by their titles, so with his name he had given his trust to them. He placed himself in their power and they approved of him for that.

'We welcome you among us, Aramin,' said Arguilo.

'I shall try to make contact with the Templars tonight when the twilight peace comes down from the sky. I must warn you, though, that you're all vulnerable to attacks from Atlantis.'

'We can arm ourselves,' growled Balio.

'This isn't a war of weapons,' Aramin warned him. 'It's a war of minds. The Templars are the mind of Atlantis and their one mind is stronger than your individual minds.'

'Then what are we to do?'

'Their weapons are to bring nameless fears into your minds. They might try to craze your children with wild dreams. They may drive your wives mad with melancholy. That is partly how they controlled Atlantis.'

'To fight them, you must strengthen your own minds. Make sure your children are happy, for happiness is the best protection against them. It will keep dark dreams from crushing them. Give them joy, fill their days with as many happy hours as you can.'

'For yourselves, keep guard on your thoughts. Speak together very often, so that you know each other's minds and can laugh away each other's fears. Direct your thoughts towards one goal and you'll be strong.'

'It's already nearing twilight,' Arguilo said.

He went alone to the prow of the craft and gazed up at the bright evening star. However, he did not really see it. He was reaching out with his mind, trying to pick up those shuddering grey vibrations which were the one mind of the Templars. Anyone watching him and hoping to discover the secret of this communication would have been disappointed. He merely stood there quietly, alone.

They waited till darkness for him. Just a few of them, the oldest captains of the Sky Fleet, sat with Arguilo in the Fleetmaster's cabin. Larn was with them, brought by Bron to share in all that was to happen. Kerin had not moved from his place beside his father.

'It may be that you'll have to be a man before your time, lad,' said Bron seriously.

So Larn sat there in company with the hard men who were captains and waited until Aramin came back to them. The men passed wine among themselves and Larn refused it, finding its bitter taste not much to his liking. The night came down black and the stars glowed brightly before Aramin returned.

The door was flung open and he at last came into the large cabin. He was pale and sweating.

'Well?' demanded Arguilo.

'Wait,' said one of the others, 'Let the poor fellow take a drink first. He's as pale as a Templar,' and they laughed, but not very surely.

They poured him a draught of wine and he drained it in one gulp. Gradually a little colour returned to his cheeks.

'Is it bad?' Bron asked him.

Aramin nodded.

'They aren't willing to talk with us unless we surrender everything and fall on their mercy.'

There was silence.

'How do we know that's true?' asked Herga. When they looked at him, he said defensively, 'Well, how do we? He stands out there by himself, doing nothing. Then comes in and tells us that. How do we know it isn't just a trick? Who knows whether he can speak with the Templars or not?'

It was true. How could they know? Such gifts were not given to the sky-people. To speak without speech and hear without ears, how could they know? They turned their gaze now on Aramin.

Bron said: 'I knew such things when I was a boy. Let him tell you how it feels to him.'

Aramin looked helpless. 'If I tell you how it feels, will that convince you? It must be like a sighted man explaining colours to the blind. I can understand you find it hard to believe that we Technicians and Templars can speak secretly mind to mind.'

'Then do they know our minds too?' demanded Herga.

'If they all turned their mind to you, everyone of them to you, perhaps they would have a good idea of what was happening in your thoughts. Not exact, but a shadow of it. But it needs two, one to send and one to receive. It needs two kinds of power. How can I explain it to you, when none of you have that power. On Atlantis we were trained to it from childhood.'

'Show it with me,' said Larn. 'When I was a little boy they started to train me before my father became an enemy, and I can still use the power when I try hard.'

Aramin looked doubtful. 'If you aren't trained fully, it can hurt you.'

'Better that you show them you can be trusted than you worry about that,' said Larn sharply.

'Very well. Go out of the room,' said Aramin. As soon as the door had closed behind him, Aramin ordered three of the captains to hand over some small personal object wrapped in a cloth so that its shape and size did not betray it. Then someone summoned Larn back into the room again.

'Stand there and close your eyes,' said Aramin. He held one of the objects in his right hand. 'Tell this man what I hold inside this cloth in my right hand.'

Larn was silent and tension quivered in the room, among the captains, and like a fierce current between the man and boy. They all saw sweat break out on the boy's forehead and he answered unsteadily: 'A whistle from the heart of the sea, from a wandering creature.' And he opened his eyes and took the cloth and carried the whalebone whistle inside unerringly to its owner. Twice more he did the same and then fell to the floor in something like a convulsion.

'It's enough,' said Herga in a low voice. 'For me anyway, it's enough.' He looked round at the others and they muttered agreement. Bron wrapped the boy Larn in a blanket and carried him to a bed.

'Precious little mercy they'd have if we gave in now,' sighed Herga.

'Those are the only terms they offer,' Aramin said.

'Then we must go on as we planned,' Arguilo returned to his theme.

'You still wish to go to the Ice Lands?' Aramin said.

'Yes. Why?'

'Marrad is heading there also. We shall be against our own people.'

'Well, he still has to prove his loyalty too,' Balio grinned.

However, the others could find little enough for mirth in the news. It meant that the two fleets would find themselves virtually at war with each other.

'I had hoped to avoid any direct meetings, if it was possible,' Arguilo muttered.

'It isn't possible,' Bron said. 'If Marrad and we are going to the same place in search of the same prize, then we are at war. And when you realise that we must get there first, at any cost, then there can be no choice.'

'I didn't want to set my people at each other's throats.'

'Don't lose heart,' Balio said. 'It's too early yet for that. Why, we don't know what the future may bring.'

'There may be better ways to travel there,' Bron suggested. 'After all, you have all the charts here—every possible chart, while the others can only have a fraction of that number.'

'That's true,' Arguilo nodded. 'I wasn't thinking. It may well be that there's a special route—a way through they wouldn't know.'

'There, you see,' said Balio cheerfully. 'We may never meet them in direct conflict after all.'

The air of the meeting lightened. Some hope had come into the room now. None of them wanted to fight their own people. Few of them really wanted even to oppose the Templars, were they honest enough to admit it. They certainly did not want to kill or injure others of their own blood. Now it seemed that careful scheming might keep them out of too much trouble.

'Lights, let's have more lights,' called Arguilo to the watchmen.

He went to the shelves which were covered with charts, pulling out one after another. Eventually, the whole table was hidden under the charts and they went through them until they had narrowed their examination to less than ten charts. These few they examined minutely, carefully following all the old voyages which had been carefully inked across the maps.

In the end they were not much cheered by their work. It

seemed that there could only be one route to the Ice Lands. Within small detours it could be varied, but each way was substantially the same. Arguilo looked tired and defeated.

'All routes will lead us both the same way in the end,' he said hopelessly. 'I don't see that we can really avoid a conflict when we come together.'

'Leave it now,' Bron said to him. 'It's late. We're all tired. We can't think clearly. Tomorrow we'll go through all the charts again. Perhaps something else will turn up for us then.'

'He's right,' Balio said. 'There's probably another way that we're too weary to see now.'

Arguilo agreed. They folded the charts and Kerin put them away until the next morning. The others left for their own craft and Arguilo walked back to his quarters with Pala. He put his arm casually about the girl's shoulders, but it was an unusual gesture of affection.

'It isn't going to be an easy time for us, my dear.'

'No one expects it, father, but they're with you in their hearts and that's the most important thing,' she said earnestly.

Arguilo smiled at her.

'Are you sorry that it's like this, Pala?'

'No, but I worry about Kerin.'

'Not becoming a Templar? It may be our saving, refusing to let him go.'

'Because now they won't be able to hurt us through him, you mean?' she said wisely.

'Yes—and that one day he will after all take my place. That's important to me, you know.'

'Mm, Bron said something like that.'

He looked at his daughter sharply. 'You talk with Bron a great deal, don't you?' Her father's voice was almost wistful.

'He's always talked to us, since we were very young.'

'And I haven't?'

Pala felt embarrassed by the conversation. There has always

been a certain distance between the twins and their father. He had too much to think about, too many responsibilities to carry, to have been able to spare them all the time they needed. When he had time alone with them, his mind was never relaxed enough for them to play with him. They had become used to acting formally with him and now this was the extent of their relationship with him. The idea that her father had other sides to him was a difficult one for Pala to accept now.

'Oh well, we always knew how much you had to think about,' she said at last and her father grinned wryly at the tone of consolation.

They walked the last few yards to their quarters in thoughtful silence. When they reached them, Arguilo paused for a while. Pala waited.

'You know,' began Arguilo.

'Yes?' Pala said politely.

'You know, parents are people too, Pala, my dear,' and Arguilo smiled and went into his cabin.

Pala crept into her own bunk and lay thinking for a long time before sleep came to her. Even when it came, she was restless. She was only just below the shadow of sleep and kept slipping very near to the surface again. Dreams twisted in and out of her mind, full of violence and flashing colours, and when she woke the next morning she ached as if she had been beaten all night long.

6

Taula sat with the Master of the Templars. Patiently he was taking down the apparently interminable formulas which the Master dictated to him. He used the quill swiftly and tirelessly and the Master watched the steady movement with pleasure.

'Ah, Taula, you have an admirable script,' he murmured after a while. Taula glanced up at his Master.

'Is there much more?' he asked politely.

'Not for now. Set the pen aside. Call the servant in and tell him we'll eat.'

Taula did as he was told. He went to the door and called up the corridor. There were running feet, for the servants knew better than to delay when the Master of the Templars wanted them for anything. Taula came back into the room.

'They'll come immediately.'

'Good. Sit down.'

They both sat at the table, the Master of the Templars gazing out of the window into the palace gardens. Dark trees grew there, and secretive shrubs through which small animals crept. There were streams too, of dark water in which eels and brown fish lived. Despite the gloomy view, the sky was still bright and this cheered the Master of the Templars.

A knock at the door.

'Enter.'

The servant came in, carrying a tray laden with food. He set out the dishes and the goblets of wine with trembling care. Then he bowed and still bowing went backwards out of the room.

'Eat,' said the Master of the Templars and Taula helped himself to the food. The Master watched him eat for a few minutes, taking a certain jaded pleasure in the young man's healthy appetite. Becoming aware of those stern eyes upon him, Taula slowly stopped chewing, his own eyes questioning.

'Master?'

'It's nothing,' he sighed. 'Finish eating.'

Guardedly, Taula cleared the plate of food. Even he, favourite though he was, had been bruised by the old man's whiplash temper.

'How goes it with the Sky Fleet, Master?' he asked, when their meal was done.

'Nothing changes—yet.'

They were silent.

'Master?'

'Well?'

'Is there nothing to be done?'

'What do you think should be done?'

'There must be something. If the Great Work were done, would it not help us?'

'I know nothing of the end of the Great Work. Only the True Lord of Atlantis could know, my son.'

'When he is done, what then?'

'I know nothing, believe me.'

At the old man's order, the servant came in and refilled their goblets. The afternoon was passing, but they were both reluctant to return to the task. For days now, the Master of the Templars had been dictating secret documents to Taula and he had been transcribing them. Formulas followed rituals, complex ceremonies followed detailed recipes and herbal prescriptions.

'Should we go on?'

'Not yet. Let's rest a while longer.'

'I little thought that when I was elected to the select company of the Templars I would sit writing like a clerk,' mused Taula, without any complaint in his voice.

'What did you think?' The old man looked at him curiously.

'I don't know. I was a child when I was named for the Templars. To tell the truth, I think my father was glad enough to be rid of me.'

'And your brothers—what of them?'

'They cared little enough for me either. To them, I was just a child, no good for their games. For myself, I longed always to be able to read. I thirsted to know things which none of my family knew about. I must have seemed oddly out of place there among merchants.'

The Master of the Templars listened to Taula's tale which closely echoed his own origins. Perhaps that was the bond between them. Certainly this young man, humble though he was, had always seemed to be drawn to the Master of the Templars. It was he himself who had fought to be taken on as his pupil and, when the Master could not break his spirit, he decided to use it instead. An arrangement which seemed satisfactory to them both.

'I was the child of a herbalist. They had almost given up hope of children when I was born to them,' said the Master and Taula listened in surprise at this unexpected confidence, 'Then when I was taken for the Templars, they wept for losing me again.'

'Why do so many of the Templars come from humble parents, Master?'

'I don't know. The True Lord of Atlantis seeks us out according to our merit—'

'And according to his purpose?'

'Possibly.'

The Master's answer was short, and Taula realised that he had questioned too closely.

There was also another reason, which the Master could not comment upon without being accused of treason, and he would not be foolish enough to lay himself open to such an accusation. As long as the Templars came from such a widespread field of origin, no one family could hold power in the land. The True Lord of Atlantis was wise enough to guard against such an obvious threat to himself as the building of an aristocracy.

'The boy will not be lost to us now?' He suddenly changed the subject.

'From the Sky Fleet? I think not. He is ours. Somehow he'll still come over to us. The True Lord of Atlantis never loses his own.'

'Will we break him?'

'We shall,' then the Master looked at Taula warningly. 'But you will learn that which you are allowed to learn.'

Taula took the reproof and asked no more. He had learned swiftly when to push and when to wait and it was that which kept him so long in favour.

'Come, let us get this weary task done,' sighed the Master of the Templars.

Throughout the afternoon they worked, steadily going through the decaying pile of old and mildewed manuscripts.

'You should be proud, Taula,' said the Master. 'Every one of these goes to the True Lord and he reads through each one.'

Taula shot an odd sideways glance towards the Master, but it went unnoticed. Nevertheless, the old man registered the fact that he cared nothing either for praise or blame. Not that he left much space for blame.

'I sometimes wonder where we are going,' said Taula, not looking up from his work.

'We are bringing together all the research that has gone into the Great Work so far. It may be that the Great Work will be completed soon.'

'That would be a fine thing for us,' said Taula in an unemotional tone.

'It may be.'

'I thought—we all thought—that it was the task of centuries. When I was brought here as a young boy, it was all the talk of the Templars.

'It has already been the task of centuries. It must come to an end sometimes—perhaps then in our own time. Who knows?'

'Master?'

'Yes?'

'When the Great Work is finished, do we know what will happen, Master?' asked Taula.

'What do you think will happen?'

'They used to say—when I came here as a lad—they said that the world would stop when the Great Work ended. That the heavens would open. That the seas would boil and the skies be overturned.'

The old man smiled and shook his head. 'How can I answer you? I have told you time and again that I do not know, and you must believe me. I know little more than you, and one day you may know far more than I do.'

'I can't imagine a time when all this search would end,' Taula pushed.

'Then don't waste time thinking about such things. Instead, go on with this simple task—or is it too boring for you to spend your time upon?' said the Master sharply and Taula bent his head to the task again.

When the evening approached, they stopped working. Taula put away the quill and his silver ink-holder, stretching his fingers achingly against the cramp.

The Master stood up and went out into the corridor. It was time for the evening ceremony, the one time when the True Lord of Atlantis came into their company. At this hour the House of the Templars was forbidden to anyone not of the company of the Templars. If any unfortunate was ever found wandering the corridors, which was a rare enough occurrence, he was executed instantly. By such grim measures, it was ensured that no one in Atlantis found out about the identity of their real ruler.

The night came down suddenly, as it did in that part of the world, and the sky was soon black. As the day died, the ceremony in the Temple began, and the True Lord of Atlantis led the celebration of the night.

He came in last, into the assembly of Templars dressed in their robes of starlight, shimmering darkly. He was flanked on either side by the seven Templars of the highest rank, the Magicians. Behind them, clad in shining robes black as a raven's wing came the Master of the Templars to lead the chanting.

The True Lord of Atlantis began. Standing before them, watched by all those glittering eyes, he named the name of every creature living on Atlantis. Then he spoke the seasons and their rhythms, and after that the years and their histories. Then, coming into the chant with them, he sounded each man's name who lived upon Atlantis and they echoed him, thus claiming every living man upon that land unto themselves.

Last of all he named each one of them, and made them his and helpless in his power, and then the ones that were to be among their company. By this magic, of naming things by their secret names, he drew all power to himself and chained them.

As the ceremony ended, with an invocation to the mighty powers of the night and the creatures of all the dark worlds, he left them and left the echo of his power shimmering and vibrating deeply about them and through them.

7

'AND how is he—our Chosen One?'

'All is well.'

'A constant miracle. But we must work hard for him in these next few months. I feel our time may be approaching.'

'At long last.'

'Sometimes I still worry about him.'

'Why should you worry? We've done everything to offer protection, used all our power, and our powers are very great. Can you doubt that?'

'No, but think of all that's been seen and done. Men sacrificed on altars of blood. Babies slaughtered for their hearts. All the abominations of hell called up for use of their foul powers. He has talked with monsters. He's been cursed into ten thousand forms of death and terror by those creatures of night. He must be full of it—the horrors, the blood, the stench of fear, the sickly smell of decay, the hungry ghosts of the soul. Look how many times he has come to us and asked to be released from his oath.'

'And we have refused and sent him back each time. We told him that we have waited ten thousand years for him and that he couldn't set the burden down now.'

'The last time that he came, he said he couldn't face the evil day after day and not be touched by it.'

'There is no evil in him. We have looked into his heart,' a young initiate said anxiously.

'But how can he not be touched by it?'

'He must go into the heart of their evil—how else can we get there to destroy it?'

'But what about the things he has done? What about the evil he has committed to get into that heart and be trusted by them?'

There was silence, for they knew he would have to pay for it.

'It is written,' sighed the old man, staring sadly with his blind eyes. 'Every deed, whether good or evil has its debt and when payment is required, it must be paid.'

'What will he do with his double burden?'

No answer was made.

8

BRON came across Pala and Larn sitting in the shade of the deck. They looked very contented for two people living under threat and he scowled at them. It seemed that Pala was never on her own these days. Larn was always there, like an obedient shadow. Larn smiled at him but Pala looked at him warily, for she could feel his antagonism.

'You don't look as if you slept very well,' said Larn.

'I didn't,' Bron answered brusquely.

He sat down with them, fully aware that he had put a stop to their conversation. They were all silent for a while.

'Have you been in on the conference this morning?' asked Pala at last.

'Yes.'

'What have they decided?'

'Well, we're going to the Ice Lands through the Forbidden Country.'

Pala stared at him in amazement and he recovered some of his good humour. Larn merely looked interested, but then, as he was basically a land-man, he could hardly be expected to understand the full significance of Bron's announcement.

'But, Bron, how can they? We'll all be killed!' she said in horror.

'What is the Forbidden Country?' asked Larn.

'Well, it's much more than a country really, isn't it?' said Pala, turning to Bron for confirmation.

'Oh yes, it's big enough to be a whole continent. In fact, some people say it covers half the world. We don't know how big it is because we aren't allowed to travel over it.'

'Who forbids it?'

'I don't know exactly. It's a longstanding tradition. They say the Forbidden Country is guarded by mysterious creatures who fly with flames coming from their eyes and mouths. The grandfather of your grandfather's grandfather once led the fleet on a voyage into the Forbidden Country, and half the fleet was lost. They said they fell out of the sky in flames.'

Larn considered this for a while.

'But perhaps it's only a story, like the stories that tell us Atlantis was once the home of the wise men.'

'But there were wise men in Atlantis once,' said Pala.

'Perhaps,' Larn shrugged.

'So there must have been firebreathing creatures who killed our ancestors,' put in Pala, 'so how can they talk of going into the Forbidden Country?'

'Because we must. If we go round the Forbidden Country and take the old route to the Ice Lands, we shall meet the rest of the fleet and we may be killed anyway. Your father says that it's very possible that the fiery creatures are extinct now. No one has seen them in living memory.'

Larn still did not look disturbed by Bron's words but Pala knew the full importance of them.

'I don't see why you look so worried,' he said.

'That's because you aren't one of us,' Pala said coldly and Larn flushed and bit his lip.

A group of sailors passed them, talking animatedly. It soon became obvious from their words that they had not seen the little group sitting under the shadow of a raft.

'Mebbe he's gone mad – who knows but the Templars haven't laid their influence on him,' grunted one of them, the faithful bosun of the master ship.

'Could be in their pay, even. It seems like anything could happen these evil days,' said another.

'Shame on you!' scolded the first mate. 'If I had my way, I'd cut your hearts out and feed them to the birds! I didn't think to hear treason on my own craft.'

'Come now, friend, we've crossed a hundred seas together,' said the bosun. 'Can you say your captain's doing right this time? What he's after is to feed us all to the fiery beasts—not just our hearts, but our souls and bodies complete!'

'Either that or he's gone mad,' said the other.

At that moment, the first mate caught sight of them sitting there, listening with open mouths to their conversation. He grinned at them, but something in his face told them how badly he felt his shipmates' words. The others grew suddenly quiet and they passed without another word.

'There you have it,' said Pala firmly. 'If father's own people feel like that, how can he hope to keep them all with him?'

'You don't understand and neither do they. There isn't any· other way. We can't fight our own people. Even if they've stayed with the Templars, they're ours. They're of our blood. Their hearts are like ours. Not like the land-men. So we have to go across the Forbidden Country because anyway there's a good chance that such animals don't really exist there now.'

'If they ever did,' put in Larn.

They looked at him thoughtfully, uniting against him quite unconsciously, simply because they were of the Sky Fleet and he was a land-man. Even Pala, who was rapidly coming to care greatly for the newcomer—even she excluded him at this moment.

'But it's in our tradition,' said Bron, as if that answered him. Indeed, as far as they were concerned, it did.

The Sky Fleet was infused with a frantic activity as they prepared to leave for the Ice Lands, going by way of the Forbidden Country. For everyone, not only the doubters, it was an exciting thought. At last, they would see something of that mysterious continent which they had always before now avoided. The crafts seemed to buzz with interest as people hurried to make the final preparations.

Larn found himself left very much to his own devices now. Kerin was with his father Pala had her own duties on such occasions as these. She was busy tethering the animals safely in the hold. The first moments of flight were always rough and all the animals had to be made fast in case they should be injured. Bron was in the Fleet Master's cabin, setting out the proper charts for the journey and making sure all the instruments were working correctly.

Aramin joined Larn on deck. He saw the boy's unhappy face and knew something of what he must be feeling. Casually he sat down beside him.

'I expect you feel out of all this,' he said without preamble.

Larn looked at him gratefully, glad to have someone acknowledging his natural feelings. He nodded.

'So did I when I first came to the Sky Fleet. I used to watch them and wonder what they really felt about things. Of course, as a Technician I had quite a good idea of what they thought, but I never could quite get into their hearts. I still can't.'

Larn stared at him as if he had just spoken treason and Aramin laughed.

'Oh, it's true. Even though I ally myself with them, I know I shall never be one of them. I wish I could. I dare say you wish it too, but we're different.'

'I can't forget!' Larn burst out, surprising himself by his anger. 'I can't forget all those things that happened.'

'You won't either. Believe me, I know how you feel. We've been touched by the shadows of Atlantis and we'll never entirely rid ourselves of them. You and I will always have that darkness in us.'

'Then what's the point of all this?'

'That our own children may not know that darkness,' said Aramin gently.

'Is that enough reason?' said Larn bitterly.

'You may not think so just now. The young are very self-centred,' said Aramin, himself still a very young man, 'but later on, when you begin to think in terms of others—or at least, one other—you'll understand then why it's necessary to fight to change the future.'

They were silent for a few moments. Then Aramin roused himself to work.

'I must go to the flight cabin,' he said.

Larn looked at him and sighed.

'I wish there was something I had to do.'

'I'll speak with Arguilo. There'll be something for you. Try not to brood too much.'

He turned back just as he was about to leave.

'I knew your father, Larn. He was an honourable man.'

Soon, the deck was cleared of any debris which had been left lying about and the other craft were suspended about them. They were all waiting for the signal from the master ship. The crew gathered on the deck. Arguilo came up to join them. Gradually, the master ship drifted out before the others. A yellow and orange flag was raised up the rigging. Gently and then more fiercely, the craft took flight. Then, the easy drift of the past few days was over and the Sky Fleet started on the voyage to the Ice Lands. The fleet cut speedily through the air and a low-pitched humming sounded in the air about them.

'There!' said Pala enthusiastically gripping Larn's arm. 'We're off at last! Now you'll see how beautiful it is to live with the Sky Fleet!'

They moved into a stately procession, slicing through the still air with no tremor of their massive rigging, just the sigh of their own wind. In the far distance, on a horizon almost too far away to see, lay the Forbidden Country and whatever might be waiting there. Behind them lay Atlantis and whatever threat it held for them.

Larn and Pala leant over the edge, both gazing ahead into the bright sky. Small clouds scudded above them, just tiny white clouds containing no hint of troubling weather. Bron came up from the main cabin to stand there with them, enjoying the old excitement that a new voyage always brought. This time, however, there was something else—an apprehension which he could not shake off him.

'Will it be all right?' Larn was pleading with him, but even for that he could not lie.

'I hope so, boy,' said Bron seriously and the threat was there again.

Nevertheless, the first few days of the voyage went very smoothly. The weather held and the sun continued to blaze down on them. They grew calm, feeling that all threats were holding off from them.

Only Pala had anything to complain of, and she could find no real words for it. Just that every night her sleep was torn by vicious and frightening dreams. No one else seemed to suffer from it. Only her. Larn kept asking her what was wrong because he could feel the tension in her. Kerin watched her anxiously.

'I don't know,' she said, shaking her head. 'I can't sleep.'

Bron noticed her pale face and reported it to her father.

'Perhaps they're reaching her,' Arguilo said, looking worried. 'The Templars?'

'Aramin said that'd be one of their weapons, to get into our minds.'

They called Pala up to them, and Aramin was with them.

'What are these dreams like?' asked Aramin gently.

Pala was annoyed by all their concern and resented being made to feel foolish.

'They're just dreams.'

'Can you tell me what you dream about?'

'Nothing definite. Just noise and colours and feelings.'

'What feelings?'

'I feel afraid when I wake up, but I don't know why.'

They all looked at each other now.

'It could be,' said Aramin. 'I'll try to help the girl.'

He disappeared into his cabin for some hours and emerged carrying a small talisman. He found Pala and showed it to her. She stared at the tiny thing, a circle and six-pointed star with inscriptions on them, all made of gold. Aramin had strung a leather thong through it and gave it to Pala to wear.

'Don't take it off,' he instructed her, 'ever, at any time.'

Pala looked at him sceptically but said nothing. She just nodded and strolled away casually, leaving Aramin feeling faintly annoyed.

Just at dawn on the fifth day, the watchman was dozing as the day came up into the sky. A sailor came along and shook him awake.

'Araban, open your eyes, you fool!' he said roughly.

The watchman awoke with a start.

'What?' he started and clutched at his dagger.

'Look!' whispered the sailor, pointing into the grey sky.

They looked. There, approaching silently under the cover of the now fading darkness, were the ten craft that had remained faithful to their old masters. The watchman rang the alarm bell which would raise the ship, clanging away until there were sailors and crew all over the deck.

'What is it?' demanded Arguilo, his hair awry from sleep.

They all looked. Arguilo wasted no more time. He instructed the watchman to ring the attack signal so that everyone knew they were threatened. This would keep the women and children off the deck. The sailors went to weapons. These consisted of extremely long poles on rope supports that could be swung round and used as spears. Until now they had only been used to drive off marauding birds. They had never been turned against their own ships.

They stood there watching silently as their onetime companions came inexorably but unbearably slowly towards them. It was not just the crafts they were seeing in that hypnotic stillness as they stood on the decks. It was a confrontation with their entire history, a turning upon themselves, and there was not one of them who looked forward to the encounter with anything like excitement or the normal joy of battle which usually carries fighters on.

However, it had to be done. They knew that. And they knew how Arguilo hoped to keep the encounter as bloodless as possible. He had instructed them to use the long spear-ended poles which he had devised. These would be aimed for the enormous balloon-like skins beneath each wallowing craft. If they could puncture those, they could spill the air on which each craft was floating. This would not cause fatalities. It would merely remove the extra buoyancy which the ships needed for tackling heavy seas and rocky coastlines. This done, there would be no chance that Marrad could take his craft into the Ice Lands and their challenge would be removed.

It was not to prove as easy as that. Marrad's fleet came in higher, which was what Arguilo had hoped. However, before they swung close enough for the poled spears to do their job, Marrad ordered his men to fire explosives, and rocks came crashing through the rigging. One of the sailors wielding a spear was crushed to the deck by a falling rock. The mainmast crashed down throwing jagged fragments everywhere. The other sailors stared in shock at their companion as he threw himself about and moaned. Then they grabbed him and tried to hold him still, one taking a rag to wipe the blood from his face. His skull was laid open and he babbled and cursed as blood poured down his face. Then, as they watched, the man convulsed and died.

'Get the explosives!' Bron roared at them, as much to move them as to make an answer to Marrad. Instinctively through their shock they obeyed. They ran for the explosive store. Aramin meanwhile spoke hastily to Arguilo.

'I have the stuff you need. Here, tell them to load this in with their shot. But first, make them tie wet rags about their faces.'

Arguilo took the harmless looking particles in his hand.

'Just a few with each ball, mind you,' said Aramin.

They helped the sailors load the cannons and Arguilo pressed some of the slightly sticky particles against the balls. Aramin quickly ripped up a shirt from a clothes-line over the deck and dipped the rags in a waterbutt. He gave them to each of the sailors and ordered them to tie them round their noses and mouths. One sailor was already up the rigging, trying to tie fast the worst of the torn ropes and splintered wood until they could attend to it safely. The others were all loading the cannon and two were still bent over their fallen comrade's body as if seeking to do something for him.

'Now fire!' ordered Bron.

The cannons all roared together. Bron had ordered them to aim only at the first ships of Marrad's fleet and to get the balls on the decks, not to tear through the rigging—an order which many of the sailors could not comprehend, since a ball on the deck did little harm. But then in the next few minutes they came to understand. White smoke seemed to rise from all over the ships and at first Arguilo's crew thought they had caught fire. Then, as the smoke drifted back across their own decks, its choking pungency made them realise it was not fire but some kind of sulphurous stink. They gasped for air despite their wet rags and one or two of them passed out. They were dragged below deck, though even there the smoke crept through.

The sailors of Marrad's fleet were completely bewildered by all this. They collapsed wherever they stood, paying no heed to Marrad's frantic orders. Panic seized the few who remained conscious. Staggering across the decks, choking and gasping, their hands to their throats, they made for shelter below deck. All thought of pursuit and vengeance was gone.

'Now!' Arguilo yelled triumphantly, 'All speed ahead'. The signal was passed from one craft to another and swiftly they pulled away towards the Forbidden Country.

'Where are they going, the fools?' asked Marrad in astonishment.

'Towards that eastward land,' answered one of his men.

'But that's the Forbidden Country!' he said amazedly.

His men all stood and watched the fleet arc away from them, dragging their stricken comrades with ropes. Balio's craft followed them, limping along at the end of the ropes.

'Why have we stopped?' asked Marrad's men.

'We can't follow them there.'

'We have the advantage of them, master.'

'Nevertheless, we'll perish as well as them if we follow.'

He could hardly believe his eyes. He was pleased to watch them going on, apparently to their doom. He was disappointed not to be able to follow up the surprise attack to a deserved triumph.

However, his main feeling was one of astonishment. He could not understand why they were going into such strange territory. He knew that, even with the surprise to his own advantage, there was still a strong chance that Arguilo's fleet would trounce his own. Now, it seemed, he was left the holder of an odd victory.

His own men came up to him joyfully.

'Well, the Jewel of the Ice must be ours!' they cried.

He watched the fleet fleeing him.

'If they stop before the Forbidden Country, shall we go after them, master?' asked his bosun.

'If they do—yes.'

However, they went on into that mysterious land with no faltering. His fleet grew silent. Quietly they stared after their former comrades until they were swallowed in the mist of the horizon. Marrad sighed. The victory was his, true enough, but it made him sad somehow. Despite his years long jealousy of Arguilo this was not what he would have wanted.

He murmured, as if to convince himself: 'The Jewel is ours, at least.'

9

ARGUILO felt the sadness of seeing his people divided by battle, but he had no time to spare on such regret. His first task was to draw his fleet together at some safe stopping place so that they could find out the extent of their losses.

Kerin now saw at first hand the kind of man his father was. On Arguilo's express orders, he went everywhere with him.

'I won't have time for instruction, my son,' he had told him only the previous night. 'You must go with me. That shall be my teaching.'

So it was. As soon as they were into the mist which hid them from Marrad's people, he ordered the craft to stop. They were all linked together and he climbed up a rope ladder to Balio's craft. Balio ran to embrace him and Arguilo patted his shoulder. A weeping woman ran out to him and started to beat him with her fists, great tears pouring down her cheeks all the while. Gently the sailors held her back.

'I'm sorry,' Arguilo said to her. It was the dead sailor's wife.

'Sorry!' she spat at him. 'And will your sorrow feed my grief? Will your sorrow be father to my children?'

Two little boys clung to her skirts, themselves crying, not

because of their dead father—that they did not understand—but because their mother wept.

'Your children will not want—even for a father. I didn't want this war, not on our own people. This wasn't what I wanted.'

She looked at him with wild eyes.

'I don't care what you wanted,' she snarled. 'I had a husband. My children had a father. Now we have neither—because of your wants.'

Balio looked embarrassed by this.

'My dear,' he said gently to the woman, 'Take your children to their cabin. I'll come to see you later,' and he signalled for two of the other women to lead her away. She went without further protest.

'I didn't want this, Balio,' said Arguilo with sorrow.

'I know. Don't worry. It's a hard thing but we knew really that a clash was inevitable.'

'But if this happens now, I dread to think what will happen later when we get to the Jewel. It really will be a matter for battle then.'

'We shall be there before them.'

'If—'

'No ifs, Arguilo. Come now,' Balio patted his arm. It was a very private moment of stress for Arguilo and only Balio and Kerin were there to see it. Kerin felt both elated at the intimacy and frightened by the weakness that the moment revealed. But it passed. His father became the hard man that he felt he knew. However, a certain warmth remained, something that enabled Kerin to see the whole man, not just the father and the authority over him.

'Who was the man?'

'Daren—a good man. Young, only a few years married. We'll miss him badly, but—' he shrugged to show there was no blame.

They walked about the deck, inspecting the damage. In some ways they had been lucky. The falling masts had done very little damage. The guardrails had been smashed down but there was little enough to show for it otherwise. The masts could be replaced. Every craft carried in its hold spare masts. It was only the main mast that had no spare. Fortunately this was untouched.

'We'll keep the ropes on you until the masts are made good.'

'Fair enough. If we continue slowly, we'll make the speed up later. I just hope there'll be no need to travel fast in the next two or three days.'

'So do I!' said Arguilo grimly.

'I'll take care of this now,' Balio said.

Arguilo made his way back to his own craft, followed by Kerin. Bron came up to them.

'Much damage?'

'Less than I feared. Only one man lost—though that's one too many. No one else even hurt though. That's better than I hoped. Only the small masts are damaged and they have replacements for them.'

'Good enough. How do they take the death?'

'How would you expect?' said Arguilo bitterly. 'It was Daren they lost.'

'I know him. He was always a goodhearted young fellow. I'm sorry.'

'I too.'

Then Bron turned to Kerin.

'I think you'd better go and eat now. Your mother's waiting. Better find your sister.'

'Oh, she'll be with Larn. She always is,' he said sulkily and went off to find them.

Arguilo and Bron looked after him.

'Is that what I think it is?' asked Arguilo.

'They're very young yet.'

'These things begin early sometimes. Anyway, normally she would be married within two years.'

'Certainly he seems to feel out of things.'

'Kerin? Yes. Perhaps he imagines it though. He and Pala have always been close. Maybe too close. Sometimes we used to think so. We worried that they'd never see themselves as being two separate people. Perhaps it's happening now.'

'As long as they don't divide too much over this.'

'It can't be helped. I don't worry too much about them. It would have to happen. It's him—Larn I worry about. He's a land-man basically. I wonder if she really appreciates what that means.'

'Wait and see. They're very young. They may separate over others yet.'

Kerin did indeed find Larn and Pala together. They were talking earnestly. They were always talking earnestly. Yet when he listened to the conversations that they took so seriously, they seemed mundane enough to him. They were only of life in general. Observations of people. Even discussions about the sort of weather they each liked best. Kerin could not really see why it was important.

That it was important he had no doubt. He could feel Pala's intense interest. She had a positive hunger to find out all about Larn and he returned that attention. To Kerin, they were both boring. He already knew most of Pala's opinions and he had no special wish to know Larn's.

To the adults, of course, this acute interest in each other was immediately recognisable as being the start of the process of loving. Had Kerin known that, he would have been even more bored by them, and perhaps affronted. However, he was ignorant and so were they.

'Are you eating?' he said brusquely to them.

'I suppose so,' answered Pala in an annoyingly vague way, as if food was of no importance.

They went with him. Most people ate sparingly that day.

They were disturbed and worried about the day's events, and they were apprehensive of entering the Forbidden Country.

However, the three of them ate well enough after all and Kerin felt good-humoured again towards his sister and Larn before the end of their meal.

'How is Father?' asked Pala. She knew he had been appointed to follow him everywhere, to learn what he could.

'Oh, he's a bit concerned about everything, but not too much. I don't think so anyway.'

He made no mention of Arguilo's moment of doubt about Balio's craft. Somehow that seemed private.

'Will it be all right, do you think, Kerin?'

Larn looked at him, his mouth set straight.

'I don't know,' Kerin shrugged helplessly. 'We all hope it will, but how can we know?'

'If we fall into the hands of the Templars, I hate to think what would happen to us all,' he muttered.

A darkness came down around them.

'It's odd, isn't it,' said Kerin, 'that nothing has come from the Templars yet.'

'Except your bad dreams,' teased Larn.

She shot him a venomous look.

'No one can help dreams,' she muttered.

'Seriously, Pala, tell me what you dreamed,' he persisted.

'I don't know.'

'Tell me.'

'It was just vague things—just noise and colours and horrible feelings.'

'Something odd happened to me last night,' offered Kerin.

'What?' they both looked at him.

'It's difficult to explain. It was as if I'd been dreaming something even I didn't know about. I sort of fell into a dream which must have been going on somewhere else in my mind. It was already in full swing and I just caught the end of it.'

'Mm?' she sounded doubtful, 'Go on.'

'Well, it was like you were saying—all colours and violence and fear.'

'And what happened?'

'I woke up and lay there feeling terrified—too scared to move. Then gradually I must have gone back to sleep and it didn't happen again.'

'Perhaps you should get Aramin to make a talisman for you too,' suggested Larn.

'Perhaps Aramin should do what?' asked Aramin, suddenly appearing beside them. He sat down with them.

'He's been having my dreams,' Pala told him.

'Have you?' Aramin turned to him.

'I'm not sure,' he answered in a puzzled tone and repeated his experience to Aramin. He listened attentively.

'I see.'

'Well?' demanded Kerin.

'Well what?' Aramin looked at him.

'What does it mean?'

'Probably that you're both particularly vulnerable to the special powers of the Templars.'

'What are they?'

'Powers of the mind. You both have minds which are sensitive to outside influences. It's probably because you're used to attuning to each other mentally.'

'How do you know that, Aramin?'

'I should know. I am—or, was—a Technician. I was taught to know something of men's minds, or to find it out.'

'That's what they were to teach me,' Kerin said suddenly and he had an odd note to his voice.

'Don't place too much value on such things, Kerin. It's not such a gift. Believe it or not, there are many times when I would rather not know what is in people's hearts.'

He considered this for a while.

'Aramin?'

'Yes?'

'Don't you think it strange that the Templars have done nothing to us yet?'

'Do you know that they haven't? Besides, it may be that they hoped that Marrad's fleet would do more damage than they did. If we hadn't come on into the Forbidden Country, we would have had more losses.'

'But I'd have thought they'd know about that—about our going into the Forbidden Country.'

'I don't know. Even with my training I have no idea of the real extent of their powers. They may be much greater than any of us could imagine. Or much less. They worked so much through fear, they perhaps don't need extra powers.'

'Do you really think they could even know our every thought?'

'They may even know every thought we are going to have,' he said quietly.

Larn felt a cold chill trickle up his spine and he shivered.

'What a gloomy collection!' Bron said roughly as he came upon them. 'Was your meal that bad?'

They laughed and the relief swept their mood away, leaving only a faint shadow with them.

Balio's craft was repaired more easily than they had feared. Arguilo sent his strongest men over to help with the raising of the masts and the job was completed in a day. He knew it would take far more than that one day to repair the damage done to morale on that craft, but he had hopes even of that. Balio tried to reassure him on that count.

'There's no feeling against you, Arguilo. Don't doubt us, whatever you do.'

'As long as I can feel all my people are with me,' he said

uneasily. 'It's for their sake we're doing this.'

'They are! No one wants to return to the Templars now, not as bondmen anyway.'

'If only we had been able to speak with them—to make our oaths before them. I'm still loyal to Atlantis.'

'We know. We're with you. Even Daren's wife—she came to me this morning. She wants me to apologise to you. Even she understands, in spite of her grief. And if she is with you, well—' he shrugged.

'I hope so.'

The two men smoked peaceably together for a while.

'Balio, you know I have a land-man on my ship? A boy, rather.'

'Larn—yes, I know him. He seems a nice young fellow, if a bit sad-looking, though that's understandable.'

'I'm wondering if you can take him on your own craft. This terrible business of Daren has brought my mind back to it. I'm not really talking in terms of him replacing Daren. That wouldn't be possible. I don't want you to think that, but he should have a place and a function within the Sky Fleet. It's particularly important now. At the moment he's drifting about like a shadow with no owner.'

'I'm amenable enough to that, but what about your daughter?'

'Pala? What about her?'

'Why, don't tell me you don't know. Well, they say the family is the last to know. It's all the gossip of the women. They say she loves him.'

'Oh that! Well, it may be so. She's too young yet to have such notions. Anyway, it's not as if he'd be far away, is it?'

'Nevertheless, you may find it difficult.'

'I'm sure, Balio, that my own daughter isn't about to stand in the way of the orders I give,' Arguilo said firmly and Balio concealed a smile.

When he returned to the master ship, Arguilo sent someone in search of Larn. The boy was, as usual, with Pala. She looked slightly startled as her father's summons was delivered but Larn showed no alarm. He went quickly in search of Arguilo.

He took the news of his move with no visible change of expression and Arguilo found it hard to know what he felt.

'You'll have something to do, at last,' Arguilo said.

'Yes, sir.'

'Which will be better than hanging about idly all day.'

'Yes, sir.'

'You'd better go now.'

'Yes, sir.'

As he went, the twins' mother came in and Arguilo was suddenly startled to see how tired she was. She sat by the window and looked out across the sky.

'It's hard for you, isn't it?' said Arguilo gently. She looked around, surprised, for he was not a man to whom tenderness came easily. Out of weakness, tears came to her eyes and she shook her head angrily. He came over to her and got up beside her. They shared the silence of their sudden emotion, both surprised by it.

'You didn't marry me for this, I know, but I'm trying to make a better future for all of us,' he said uncertainly.

'Husband, we have never been weak, either of us. We've fought all the way through everything—even losing the babe.'

It was the first time she had mentioned it since that terrible winter and he gripped her hand.

'And we'll fight through this. I have never for a moment wished for a different man than you. We have made a fine life. We have children I'm proud of, even though I think we both find it hard to understand them sometimes.'

'You too?' he said. 'I thought it was only fathers who didn't understand their children.'

She laughed. 'We are too much alike you and I. To be honest,

I've sometimes wondered if our children would not have been happier with other parents than us, but still—'

'When I was a child, I thought to be an adult meant to know everything and to understand it all too. All I know now is that I was wrong to think that.'

She patted his arm.

'But you will do what you feel in your heart is right and that's the best thing.'

They sat companionably, sharing the rareness of the moment, half aware it would supply their strength for the future. Then the door burst open and Kerin was there and his parents broke their grip almost guiltily and he stared at them, feeling something he did not understand. Arguilo came to himself again, businesslike as usual.

'Kerin, perhaps you could find your sister for me,' he suggested.

He glanced at them both and his mouth tightened.

'What's wrong? What are you going to do to Pala?' he said in a hostile tone.

'It's nothing very terrible,' said his father soothingly. 'It's just that I've decided to send Larn to Balio's craft.'

'Oh.'

'You don't mind?'

'I don't, but Pala will.'

'Pala is too young to be so involved with her heart,' said his mother firmly.

'Perhaps she doesn't know that!' Kerin said sarcastically.

'Kerin!'

'It's all very well to talk about Pala like that, but it's already happened. She is already involved. She does already care. It's too late to say she shouldn't. It's too easy to say it, as if she won't feel badly just because you've all decided she shouldn't feel badly. You don't understand her.'

'And you do?' his mother sounded angry but in reality she was hurt by his words, echoing her own so closely. She could not bear Kerin to know so clearly.

'Of course I do. I know everything that Pala thinks. She's been very unhappy these past few months. She's suffered—and now you're all going to take away from her something that's made her happy for a while.'

'If you understand her so well, then please tell me why Pala's been so unhappy,' his mother said with genuine concern overlaying her anger.

'It's just hard for us to grow up and be somewhere in between being children and being adult. And especially for her.'

'Go on.'

'We used to be very close. You know that. You always used to talk about it. We often heard you. The last few months we've been growing in different directions. I hadn't really noticed before this, but I've been thinking about it—because I felt very bad about Pala being so close to Larn and leaving me out. Now I think I understand it. Maybe it's just because she'll be a woman and I'll be a man. All the same, it's hard to be two people when you've always been almost one person. That's all.'

Arguilo was moved by Kerin's words. He knew that only weeks ago his son would not have been able to say them or even to think them probably, but his wife was disturbed.

'He's old before his time,' she said later to Arguilo.

'I think children are always old before their time in their parents' eyes,' he answered.

He made no real reply to Kerin at that time. 'I'll speak to Pala,' was his only answer.

However, the night's events overshadowed any private concerns aboard the Sky Fleet.

10

THE crystal was smoky red and shadows moved across it. The White Magician watched patiently.

'Well?' said the young man. 'Well?'

'Hush,' the old man rebuked him.

'How long before you see something?' demanded the young man.

The Astrologer smiled to himself.

'Let the crystal speak in its own time,' he admonished. 'It will not lie to us.'

As they waited, the stone cleared and became pure again, as clear as mountain water.

'Now!' whispered the young man excitedly.

The pictures grew before them, moved on and changed until a whole scene was laid out before them. After an hour or so had passed, there was nothing that they did not know.

'Ah!' sighed the Astrologer contentedly, nodding as the young man whispered it all to him.

'They won't know?' asked the young man fearfully.

'The Templars? No, not them! This stone before us is the stone of truth and it is lost to them as is the Jewel Under the Ice.

No one knows where these gems disappeared to—they're lost in our own history.'

'Do they know? The Sky Fleet, do they realise?'

'Some among them. Probably they've only been told that the Templars need it for some ceremony. Most of them will have no idea what they're really doing.'

11

THEY came—expected, yet unexpected. Expected, because their traditions told them. It was on the old charts. It existed in their mind. Not in each individual mind but in their collective memory. And, when they exploded into that night no one, somehow, was surprised. Great wheels of fire, curving and spinning in the deep night sky. Crying with unearthly voices. The night sky splintered into redness round them.

For a while there was panic. The sky-people ran up on the decks. The women were screaming and terrified children cried from the craft. Even the sailors paled under those piercing voices and merciless lights. Arguilo was out there almost before the echo of the sound and light had reached below deck. Behind him, obedient as a shadow, was Kerin. Amazed, both of them, they gazed up into the broken sky.

The creatures passed far above the rigging and their flames danced blue-green-red-and-rainbow down the sky and they could feel the heat along the deck rails. Arguilo saw the fire passing harmlessly over them and he was struck by wonder at it. Kerin put out his hand as if to catch a flame but they spun above him, burning. He gasped.

'Their flames are endless!' said his father astounded, and shouted to the others not to panic.

Steadily a barely-held calmness went through them all. They grew silent and stared up into the torn darkness, entranced by the whirling display above them. Mothers quietened their crying children and persuaded them to watch the fireworks in the sky.

'What do you make of such a thing?' whispered Bron.

'Those are the creatures of our past—no doubt,' answered Arguilo.

'But can they really be harmless?'

'Their flames may be harmful, but perhaps they aren't trying to harm us anyway.'

'True enough.'

The craft were still. They made no attempt to evade the flying creatures who were obviously far more mobile than ever they could hope to be. Only an occasional shout broke the odd silence that held them all. Otherwise, they were all kept motionless, fascinated like children before a juggler.

The creatures were huge, with long snakelike bodies from which long feathery tendrils waved. They seemed to have several sets of wings and great golden eyes which shone as they swooped near enough to be clearly seen. The flames—if that was what they were—were emitted from their great wings and from the edges of the floating tendrils.

They had stopped their crying now, as if that had been some sign of alarm on their part. Now they were curious. They came closer and closer to the craft, perhaps inspecting them. They avoided them so expertly, just brushing the merest shadow of their outlines, that they could all see what a magnificent control the creatures had over their great wings.

Eventually, the creatures made off into the night again and they were all left standing there, staring into the fading reflection of that brief glory.

Bron shook his head.

'I don't know what to make of that,' he said at last. 'Were they friend or foe or neither?'

'Perhaps just inquisitive and then not worried when we seemed to offer them no harm.'

'Or perhaps they're reporting back elsewhere,' said Aramin coolly.

'Is that possible?' asked Arguilo frowning.

'Surely everything is possible?'

'Well, either way, there isn't anything else we can do just now. Let the watchmen keep watch, and let the rest of the people sleep,' Arguilo decided finally.

Bron shouted directions to the others. His voice carried easily on that night air and they obeyed.

Soon the ships were all in darkness again. There was still an air of excitement around them, but most of the sky-people had returned to their quarters below deck.

'Aramin, do you know anything about those creatures?'

'Nothing. I've never heard about them, not through all the years of my instruction. I think it's possible that even the Templars know very little about the Forbidden Country.'

Arguilo looked thoughtful.

'I'm very tired,' said Kerin hesitantly.

'I'm sorry, boy, I'd almost forgotten you. Go to your bed. I won't need you for anything more tonight.'

Wearily Kerin went to bed and left them behind to continue their talking.

Despite his tiredness, he found it hard to sleep. The same dreams came to him as before—so violent that they threw him awake time after time. By morning, he felt sick and aching, again as if he had been beaten. He shook his head miserably when the daylight came creeping into his cabin. Seldom had the sight of dawn been so unwelcome.

Nevertheless he dragged himself out of his bunk and dressed.

He was too used to rising at dawn to be able to sleep further on this particular morning. Once outside in the open air, his head cleared a little. Pala was up too and she hugged him affectionately. He was relieved, for obviously she had not yet heard the news about Larn. She shot a questioning look at him, but the moment passed.

They looked over the edge of the deck.

'Oh!' she gasped.

They had forgotten that they would be within the Forbidden Country now. It lay below them, stretching into the distance. They were not sure what they expected, but it was not this gentle expanse of misty green pastures and shining river threading away through the landscape.

'And the villages!' Kerin pointed to them.

They were too far above to see the people clearly, but they could pick out the little black ants that were people moving through the village streets. Mist hung over the whole countryside this early morning and the land was etched in the softest colours of green and blue and brown.

'It's beautiful!' sighed Pala.

Somehow, because of the whispers about this land, they had both expected dark colours and harsh landscapes, torn open by nature and twisted in upheavals beneath the land. They had not thought to come across such a gently coloured land. Even so, despite the beauty, they were also conscious that there was a mysteriousness about the country, as if the mist hid something from their sight.

'It's better than Atlantis in the early part of summer,' Larn said more factually, joining them.

'Did you expect this?'

'I don't know what I expected. Not this though. No, not this.'

They stood there a little longer, then Pala looked at Larn.

'What's wrong?' she said.

Kerin felt her own twinge of fear and he silently cursed his sister's ability to pick up moods so easily.

'Wrong?' Larn said uneasily, not looking at her. Kerin made a move to go but Pala shot out a hand and gripped him surprisingly hard, so that he could not do so.

'I know there is something wrong.'

'I wouldn't say that,' Larn began.

'What then?'

'Well, I wasn't going to tell you yet. But it seems I have to go to Balio's craft.'

'Who says you must?'

'Your father. It's all arranged,' Larn spoke dully.

What Pala minded most was that Larn was not upset by the news. This implied such a difference in their mutual attitudes that she felt betrayed by him.

'He must go there,' Kerin put in, 'What else can he do? He has nothing to do here. We haven't any room for another crew member. Balio's just lost Daren, so it's obvious he should go.'

'It isn't obvious to me,' she said furiously.

'They need him.'

'He doesn't have to go.'

'No, I don't have to. Your father said I didn't have to, but I want to.'

'You want to!'

'Well, it's true there's nothing for me to do here.'

'But what shall I do without you?'

'I'll only be on Balio's craft. It isn't as if they're sending me to Marrad's fleet, or back to Atlantis.'

'It might as well be.'

'That's silly, Pala.'

'You didn't think it was silly when you first came here.'

'I was very unhappy then.'

'And now you aren't—so you don't need anyone to wipe your

nose when you snivel now.'

There was silence. Kerin was shocked at his sister's venom. Even though he could feel that inside she was crying out in anguish he was still appalled.

'I'm sorry you think that,' Larn said with commendable dignity, 'But it's nothing to do with me.'

He walked away, leaving her there with Kerin. Suddenly, she started to sob and Kerin put his arms about here and held her as tightly as he could. There was nothing he could say. He was aware that her pain was the pain of a woman and that she was too young for it. Yet, as he had told his father, just because she was so young, that did not mean she would not feel it. It just meant that she could not cope with it.

'I love him, I love him!' she moaned, realising it at that moment.

'I know,' he said and patted her shoulder helplessly. Having never suffered in that way himself, he could not really imagine what she felt. He could only feel the echo of her pain.

Although the mood under the day was sad, Kerin was soon caught up in the activities of the ship. He could only spare uneasy moments to think of Pala who moved silently and miserably about her own duties.

Under Arguilo's eye, Kerin applied himself to the charts. It was now his task to correct the ancient maps as they passed over that almost mythological land. Of the fiery creatures in the sky, there was no further sign.

'Perhaps they are night creatures only?' suggested Bron, who was watching Kerin's work with interest.

'That's possible. On the other hand, perhaps they were only there to guard the entrance of the Forbidden Country.'

'And now we're safe, you mean?'

'Possibly.'

The two men talked idly while Kerin retraced their route, following Arguilo's instructions.

'When are you sending Larn over?'

'Sometime today, as long as it seems safe.'

Every few minutes, the day watchman came in to report upon the lie of the land beneath them, pointing out on the map where some alteration was needed. Above, on deck, they could hear feet passing to and fro among them, the irregular, lightly running feet of the children.

'They're glad enough to be out,' grunted Bron.

'Well, it's hard when they're kept in their cabins.'

The children played riotously out on the deck. They shouted and screamed and threw themselves wholeheartedly into their games. No one stopped them. The adults understood that the children needed this frantic, almost hysterical release. Their life was so far from that of the land-men. They had to be allowed their exercise in whatever way they could take it.

Although the ships were large, as far as the adults were concerned, the actual ground they covered was not very great. The children of the Sky Fleet did not know what it was to run on green fields, so they were encouraged to scramble like monkeys in the rigging. The sailors joined in their chasing games. Their mothers stood back from their rough play. It was all necessary if the severe discipline of their lives was to be continued.

All the while, the gentle hills and plains of the Forbidden Country passed below them, peacefully.

12

THE Master of the Templars blazed with rage. His eyes were bloodshot and flecks of foam shot from his mouth. His face was suffused with blood and veins stood out on his forehead. Taula watched with dread, and some interest. It seemed impossible that the Master could continue his tirade without collapsing.

'You dare! You DARE—you, of all people!' he stopped, seemingly at a loss for words.

Taula looked down at his feet and made no reply.

'You haven't anything to say?'

Taula shook his head. The Master glared at him, but he was now speechless with rage. The air quivered about him and indeed the whole of the palace was echoing with his voice. The servants scurried about the corridors, dreading that they might be summoned to his presence. It would be nothing for him to slice off someone's ear in this wild mood. Only last month, an unfortunate boy had run screaming down those very corridors, with blood flowing down his neck and over his shoulder after the Master had turned on him in anger.

This was something more, however. For all his red rage, the Master knew that there was some threat here.

He had returned from a consultation with the Astrologers

when he came upon Taula in his room. This was bad enough.
Even Taula was never supposed to go into this room without
express permission. However, worse by far, Taula had actually
been reading certain documents which were intended to be secret.
They were the Master's own diaries, the complete record of his
life since he became an initiate in the mysterious order of the
Templars.

When he swung round to confront the Master, there had been
something in his eyes—something unexpected. It could not have
been triumph. It could not, the Master told himself. And yet———.

An awkward silence grew between them. The Master eyed
Taula who stared directly at him, with no expression in his eyes.
The Master felt suddenly very weary. He was too old for this sort
of intrigue. He was an old man now. He wanted a peaceful end to
his years. He wanted to finish in glory, not to start again with the
sordid squabbling of his early years. Then he had positively
enjoyed the struggle and when he came triumphant out of it, it
seemed that there could not possibly be a sweeter victory.

'Is it all to start again?' he asked at last, his anger suddenly
deflated.

'My Lord?' said Taula.

'Are there more intrigues in this palace?'

'Among the Templars, you mean?'

'That's exactly what I mean.'

'None that I know of. You are Master of all the Templars. I
don't know of any who could dare to try to take your place.'

'Then what are you doing here?'

'I wanted to know more about the Great Work.'

'Is that all?'

'All? Surely it's the culmination of all we're doing, Master?'

The Master nodded, but he felt more like weeping with relief.
As long as that was all! Just a pupil's over-zealous search for
knowledge—that he could cope with easily. It was a simple
matter of discipline.

'You know that my anger is righteous, don't you, Taula?'

Taula bowed his head, saying nothing.

'I shall have to punish you for this. Anyone else I would have executed, but I shall be merciful to you. You are to go to the crypt of the Temple where you'll find a silver whip hanging up. You shall stay there all night and flog yourself for your presumption. I'll come down to you tomorrow morning and if your back isn't raw, I'll put a slave to flog you truly.'

Taula went out of the room, silently. The Master sat down and laid his head on his hands. A red-flecked mist rose before his eyes when he closed them. He was growing old. He could feel age creeping under his skin. It was flowing cold along his blood.

More and more he was looking with the backward sight of old age, instead of the forward sight of the younger man. His early days had been full of danger and excitement and he won dark victories of blood and terror—a brilliant young man ruthlessly carving his way to power. His triumphs—the banishing of an old man to a barren land, the secretly arranged murder of a rival, the torture and betrayal of a Magician—were not so fine now that he was an old man himself in danger of secret murder and young men plotting.

He shook his head. He should rid himself of these fears. They were unhealthy. Worse, they were unfounded. They would weaken his essential powers of concentration.

'But that look on his face!' he muttered.

Perhaps he should watch Taula? Surely not? He had spent all his time, all his hopes, on that young man. Even though—or perhaps because—he knew that one day Taula would hold greater powers than he could ever hope to possess. Now, perhaps the day of renunciation was coming sooner than he expected. It was foolish to presume—as he had done—that Taula would not come into his own inheritance until the Master's death. It was foolish to have trusted him.

He summoned a servant into the room. The man approached

him smiling a forced smile which did not hide his fear.

'Lord?' he said, bowing low.

'Bring Menula to me,' he said harshly.

The servant hastily bowed and left the room. Meanwhile, the Master was left to his painful contemplations and his own fears. He had been promised mastery over death and hell by the True Lord of Atlantis. Instead, he had reached his seventieth years in chains to ritual and searching for the key to unknown knowledge. He had not yet been given that mastery—sometimes he had even questioned in his heart whether the True Lord had it to give—and already death was encroaching into his blood and bones.

But what mattered now was that he still held. He would stake all on holding his hard-won supremacy to himself. He would not lose the fragile peace of his position as the Master of the Templars, certainly not to a simple clerk.

He sat there in his room as the darkness came down on the day and did not light the lamp nor call a servant to do it for him. Because the previous day had been a festival, there was no ceremony of homage this night. The True Lord of Atlantis would be gathering up his strength again after the intensive ceremonies.

Eventually there came a sharp rap on the door.

'Come,' he said.

The door opened and Menula entered.

'You wanted to see me?' he said without preamble.

The old man nodded wearily.

'I can't see anything in here,' Menula grumbled. 'Can't I light the lamp?'

'If you wish.'

'I do wish.'

Menula struck a spark and fired the wick. The oil caught and a rich yellow glow filled the room. The old man closed his eyes against the shock of the sudden light. When he opened them, Menula was already seated comfortably in a chair, his massive legs spread out before him.

He was huge, an explosion of flesh and muscle that posed a nameless threat to those who saw him. Menacing, powerful, assured of outer strength, and some inner force that seemed greater than all the rest. His hands and feet were giant-sized. However, it was not any of these features that marked him most in people's minds. It was his face—a soft fleshed evil face, even in repose. His eyes were tiny, though keen, and his mouth was twisted downward in a thick bitter line. His nose was broken and mis-shapen, and the sum of these features—and the mind behind them—was ugliness of flesh and spirit. People shuddered when he strode past them.

Darker still were the rumours about him. It was said that he had strangled people with those gnarled hands, had torn young babes helpless from their mother's arms. It was reported that Menula had thrust living people into fires and laughed while they died burning.

In short, where Menula walked, so too did death and corruption. That was the kind of man that the Master of the Templars called to him in his doubt. He had no fear that Menula would speak of this visit. He did not doubt his discretion. No one really knew what terrible secrets Menula guarded, for he guarded them well. Their words would remain private.

Neither did Menula fear him. Menula feared no man. He did not even fear the True Lord of Atlantis, surely the only man on Atlantis who could boast such a thing. However, he did not boast of it.

'Menula is untouchable,' the True Lord of Atlantis had said once to the Master. 'There will be a special place in hell kept just for him. He is so purely evil that nothing above hell will ever touch him. He will be saved from men by his unholiness.'

'Well?' said Menula.

'I want no deeds of you yet. I want you to find something out.'

The Master of the Templars bent close to him, outlining the

nature of his request while Menula's tiny eyes watched him shrewdly.

When he finished, Menula laughed and the Master shook his head.

'You have a black heart, Menula.'

'It's true enough,' the giant said complacently.

'Do you have no fear of shadows?'

'None.'

'I don't think I would wish to have your confidence, not if it meant sharing the burden of your deeds.'

'Why do you shiver? What do you have to fear?'

'While we live there is always fear.'

'Not for me.'

'Perhaps you're right. For you, what comes after death is more important.'

'I have no fear of that either. What I have given, I can take.'

'For eternity?'

'If need be.'

'Well, what else have you to tell me?'

'That he trusts me.'

'And you will betray him?'

'When the time comes.'

'That's all I wanted to know.'

'I'll tell anything more there may be when the time comes.'

'Until then, let no one see you come to me.'

'Don't worry.'

'Farewell then.'

'Farewell.'

Menula went into the night watched from the shadows by Taula who played with an amulet, sliding it through his fingers, a little smile of triumph on his face.

Later the messenger came to the blind Astrologer.

'Go to the White Company,' he said. 'Let them know that the wheel turns.'

'And no one knows?'

'Why ask? You of all people know how well versed we are in treachery,' said the messenger bitterly. 'Why should we fail now?'

'Don't let bitterness into your heart. You know it must be done. It's the only way that we can bring the true heart of Atlantis to life.'

'But at the cost of so many deaths and betrayals. And we aren't at the finish yet.'

The old man was silent, thinking.

'There are no absolutes,' he said. 'There isn't any way of achieving what we must achieve without all this evil. Atlantis is riddled with evil and we must use its own evil against it. You know it is our teaching that if the ultimate good can be achieved even through evil, then our commitment must be to that end.'

'And I must pay for it! For a burden that I never asked to bear, old man. Where is the justice in that?'

'The burden is great because the reward will be great. Believe that. We count on you. Not just us, not just the few hundred members of the White Company, but all the rest. All the lost generations of Atlantis who went into darkness through torture and nightmare. All the children of our children who would otherwise been born into the darkness. If you fail us now, how many hundred years more do we have to wait for another one to take up the burden?'

There were tears on the old man's cheeks.

'Have no worries,' said the messenger more gently. 'I'll keep the burden you gave me.'

'If you fail us, there will be everlasting dark on Atlantis.'

13

DARKNESS. Quiet. An easy night. A sharpness in the air overlaying the warmth of the day. Stars bright, seeming to be so near that they were only just out of reach. The craft itself creaking in flight. Far below, the lights of a mysterious country, marking homes and warming fires.

Pala watched, disturbed by the beauty of the night. She was still sad, yes, but the melancholy had some distance from her now, as if there were some deeper part of herself that could not be moved by mere emotion. Someone else moved to the deck and stood, like her, staring out at the night.

'Fine night this,' said Bron.

Pala nodded. A burst of laughter came from the watchmen, joking among themselves.

'People always find something left to laugh about,' he observed, and she knew that he understood what she was feeling.

'However sad they are?'

'Yes, that's human nature. However miserable a man is, he still has to admit that some things are funny and some are beautiful. They don't change because he changes.'

'It doesn't mean he doesn't care?'

'Oh no, it just means that he understands that there isn't only him and his view of things in the world. Most people learn it sooner or later. Some learn it early in life, and some later. I suppose there are a few that never learn.'

They were silent, a sharing between them. She knew suddenly it was finished—a brief fire that had flared and died.

'Bron?'

'Mm?'

'Have you ever lost someone you thought you loved?'

'Most people have, my little chick.'

'But have you?'

'Yes, I have too.'

'And was there a time when it didn't hurt so much?'

'Yes—there was, eventually.'

Then he went on, as if to himself.

'After she died, I cried. Me, a grown man! Weeping like a baby, night after night. I used to sit there holding her clothes sometimes, pretending that she was still there.'

She held her breath, not daring to interrupt his privacy.

'Then, one night, I was standing on deck like this, but it was far away from here. Right up in the cold regions. Suddenly we came on a school of great white fish. We drifted over them, and there they were—beautiful kingly creatures, just taking their own course.

'I watched them for hours then we were far in front of them and they were out of sight. Then I remembered my grief again. But after that it wasn't so bad. I knew I'd recovered. Of course, I won't ever forget, but I'd learnt that the world goes on—and that's a hopeful thing, not something to despair about.'

She listened to him because he had a right to tell her time would heal. He had found it so.

Exploding out of the peaceful dark they came again. This time, as they swooped down on the fleet, there was another horror with them. There were riders clinging to their shining weaving bodies.

Men with swords, leaning down over the decks as the fiery creatures came low.

Chaos broke loose. Sailors ran for their weapons and it came to hand to hand battle, between the fiery riders and the men of the Sky Fleet and all the scene was lit with the eerie flamelight from the creatures.

The children were thrust below deck and the women put with them. They shrieked and sobbed in their fright and the captains tried to keep them stilled, to ease their panic. Meanwhile, the children gazed through windows up at the miniature of hell being fought on their own ships. Most of them were too young not to enjoy the spectacle. It was like one of their own traditional tales. The armoured riders screaming their battle cries, the sailors vainly trying to bring down the riders of their mounts. Kerin stood in the shadows and watched and Pala crept up there with him.

'You should be below!' he scolded.

She slid her hand into his. 'I can't. They're all right down there. The women are afraid but the children don't understand. I felt you up here. I wanted to be with you.'

He squeezed her hand.

'Are you afraid?'

'No, I'm like the children. It's too unreal somehow.'

And she was right. She could not find much horror in the scene because it was all so strange to her. Even the blood looked false.

'You should be frightened,' he said soberly. 'We may not win.'

Several of the sailors were wounded, but none seriously. They bled freely from flesh wounds but the riders could not wield their mounts easily enough to lay in a mortal blow. The creatures were too big. There was too much danger of them being trapped in the rigging if they came too low. On the other hand, neither could the sailors manage to unseat the riders.

After some time of this unsatisfactory conflict, the riders wheeled in their mounts and swung away into the sky again. The sailors watched them go, leaning over to see them weave away into the darkness of the land below.

'Is anyone hurt?' asked Arguilo, sheathing his own sword in the decorated scabbard.

'Only slightly,' answered the bosun.

Arguilo spoke to each of the injured men. It was as the bosun said. Flesh wounds, grazing and neat cuts across their hands and arms. Kerin came over from the shadows, Pala behind him.

'What are the chances of them returning?' asked Kerin.

'I don't know,' said his father.

He called them together and ordered the women and children to stay together in the big centre hold. 'Then, if the dragons should return, we shall have you all in one place and you'll be easier to look after.'

They began to move down into the hold which housed the animals. The cow and her two calves stared at them with amazement in their liquid eyes. The chickens spluttered indignantly and the cats came out of the shadows to eye them curiously.

It took very little time to settle the women and children there. Some of the children cried with weary rage at being wakened, but once they were wrapped up in blankets again by their mothers, they soon dozed off into sleep again. Pala settled with the bosun's wife, holding one of her redheaded twins in her arms. Soon the air was filled with the mumblings and sighs of many people sleeping.

14

FEAR moved into the Master's sleep, filling an empty dream with night. Shadows reaching to the skies, stormdark and screaming, and suddenly blood streamed down the horizon and over him until he woke up choking.

He lay there until the coughing fit passed. Wakeful now. A lamp glowed dimly in the room. In the corridor a guard passed. A nightbird called once sharply out in the palace grounds. All was well.

Nevertheless, sleep would not come again. He sat up and sighed. Now it would be like the other nights—a long wakefulness until the dawn, then a brief restless sleep before the servant came to wake him.

Restlessly he reached out for the intricately carved ivory pipe. Hesitated. Took it up, resigned, into his hands. It was already charged and he held a metal rod in the lamp until it glowed, then stuck it in the pipe. Soon the charge was glowing too and he began to draw into his lungs the sweetly acrid smoke.

'An old man's sleep!' he muttered, full of self-contempt, but allowing himself to be soothed into a state of ease by the fruit of the white flowers.

'This is how it ends,' he sighed. 'An old man's drugged sleep to keep the fears at bay.'

While the old man slept uneasily, Taula walked in his room. He strode to and fro, up and down, like a caged animal made sick by its bars.

It was hard for him. He was ruthless in what he had to do, yes but he had some love and much respect for the Master of the Templars. Impossible not to when he knew the old man so well, enough to measure both his weakness and his strength. Now he had to strike him down. But something else took him over at that minute. A strange mood which he could not stop or resist or ignore. A desire to look again upon the old man, to see what he knew was there, as if it might have changed and there might still be time and ways not to do the inevitable.

Before he could stop himself, he left his room and strode up the corridor. When he reached the old man's room, he threw open the door and went in. He was acting as if he were in a dream, compelled to do something beyond his power to refuse. He went over to the Master's bed and looked down on the old man as he lay there.

He looked defenceless, almost naked, in his sleep. He was just an old man sleeping, snoring with an open mouth. Suddenly, horrifyingly, the old man opened his eyes.

'What is it, Taula?' he asked, surprisingly gently.

'I didn't mean to wake you,' he stammered.

'I felt your presence cutting right through my sleep.'

'I'm sorry.'

'You haven't answered my question.'

The old man gazed at him and there was a moment of truth between them, in which Taula knew that he was discovered and the old man suddenly recognised what he had half-known all these years. He had nursed disaster all that time and now they were both sick with the truth of it, helplessly driven to fulfil their destined roles.

'So you are the one to betray me,' he said and there was no hint of a question in the statement.

'Master!' the young man threw himself down beside the bed, weeping, clasping the old man's dry hand between his own.

'You must do what is written for you to do.'

'I don't want ...'

'Then you have a better nature than ever I did. There was no sorrow in me for my treachery,' sighed the old man.

Then he added: 'Remember only this—that there is no deed without its price to be paid. One day the price will be asked you.'

'That I know also—' Taula answered sadly, tears trickling down his cheeks.

The old man wiped his tears away as gently as if he were a child.

'Go now and do what must be done. Shed no more tears for me.'

Taula made no answer. He kissed the old man's hand and laid it tenderly on the coverlet.

When the door closed on him, the old man lay back. He was quite still and his eyes were still on the door. Oddly enough, now that he knew the worst, he felt at ease. A kind of peace had come to him. That night he slept soundly for the first time in months, perhaps years.

*   *   *

They were already in sight of the mountains now and heading towards them at a good rate. Their need was urgent for two main reasons. They feared that the dragon riders would return now that the Templars realised they had been led astray, and also there was a shortage of water. They had little time to lose but they were going more slowly because the river was narrowing as it came nearer to its source.

'Isn't there anything we can do to hurry them up?' said Arguilo.

'Nothing,' Aramin said. 'What Bron told you originally is right. The speed is dependant upon the body of water you're travelling over. As the river gets smaller, you'll go slower and I know of no way round that.'

'Water's getting short now, captain.'

'I know that!'

'I'm sorry.'

'No, I'm the one who's sorry. It's just all getting to be serious for us. If they come after us now—'

He let the sentence hang in the air. At that moment, a sailor ran down from the deck, hardly even pausing to knock before he burst into the room.

'They're back!' he cried.

There was no need to ask who they were. Arguilo went up on deck and ordered everyone to shelter except for the sailors needed to man the decks.

They swooped down as before but this time the riders bore flaming torches in their hands.

'They're trying to fire us!' shouted Bron!

'Get the water tanks out here!'

They ran to man the tanks, sliding them out of their brackets on the bulkheads, ready for easy access. The riders swung down over the ships and flung the torches to the decks and rigging. As far as possible they snatched up the torches and tossed them back over the side. The dragons still blazed with fire but it was the strange flickering fire that seemed to have no heat in it. One of the sailors ran screaming across the deck, his hair ablaze. Bron grabbed him and ducked him headfirst into one of the water tanks. The sailor stood there, sobbing with pain and shock.

'Take him below,' Bron cried to another man and the sailor was led away trembling.

Little flames were nibbling at some of the rigging and sailors were clambering up to try to douse them. As they did so, the riders tried to pick them off with their long slim swords.

The craft were progessing with painful slowness. It was almost impossible to decide whether they would reach the mountains before the dragon riders managed to fire them.

'Isn't there any way to speed up?' groaned Arguilo.

'Patience, we're almost in the shadow of the mountains. Take them up—not through the pass. Take them right up over the range,' ordered Aramin and Arguilo obeyed him blindly.

Steadily the ship rose over the rocks and the mountain sides fell away beneath them. It was cold here. They were approaching the shadow of the peak. Still the riders rode determinedly with them. One of them was thrown to the deck, laid low by a cunning throw of a dagger. Two sailors threw themselves upon him, pinning him down while his forsaken mount set up a wail of loss.

One by one the craft followed the master ship. They were going more slowly now. The river was reduced to a trickle, the tiny spring where the great river had its source.

'We won't make it!' Bron cried despairingly.

'We will, we will,' shouted Aramin. 'Look behind you now!'

The riders were falling back slightly. The dragons were slowing now, involuntarily. The sailors were gasping with effort of wielding their swords. Blood throbbed in their heads. Their lungs hurt. The craft rose higher up the huge wall of rock.

'We can't go over before them,' gasped Arguilo, holding his throat painfully.

'Look!' Aramin grabbed hold of his arm, forcing him to turn round to watch the riders.

The dragons were falling away, their flames dimmed to almost nothing. Many of the riders were slumped over their necks, clinging on as if they were only half-conscious.

'Look!' Aramin pulled him round to look at his own ship. One by one the flames along the rigging were flickering out, as they were dying on the deck wherever they had taken hold.

'What's happening?' Arguilo managed to say, as he tried to gulp air into his bursting lungs. Redness spun before his eyes. A roaring sounded in his ears. Still the craft rose and now, suddenly, they could see over the mountain side to the great plain which led to the sea, not too many miles away.

'It's the height. No air,' gasped Aramin joyfully. 'Fire can't burn. They can't breathe. Too much effort to fight. Safety.'

They clung on to the deck edge, trying desperately to pull air into their starving lungs. Gradually, the ships dropped over the edge of the range. Then more rapidly, they fell, down into the rich oxygen-filled air of the lower ranges. At last, they could breathe again easily.

'We're over!' cried Bron triumphantly. 'We're over the range!'

15

It was the night of the Ceremony of the Moon. The Moon was the only mistress of the Magician-Templars, the Magicians were not permitted to marry lest they become caught up in worldly matters. The Moon took to herself treachery, evil deeds and secret betrayals as well the hunting in the dark, and women's pains. Each month the Magician Templars led the body of the Templars in an act of worship.

It was a beautiful act of adoration. The altar of the Temple was ranged with the heavy-scented flowers that bloomed at night and the Templars gathered in their splendour there before the altar. They greeted her with the rise and fall of their plainsong chants and wove a curtain of melancholy sound for her. Then, as she rose and took her rightful place in the sky, the song grew into something rich and strange. Finally, she appeared in majesty before the window open to the skies and all her beauty spilled silver across the stone of the altar as their song reached its climax. Breaking like the tides she drew across the world, falling out like the light she threw across the sky, the ritual chant ended on a note pitched high into the night.

A silence held and then an unearthly shriek was heard which turned them pale and shaking. They looked at each other. Said nothing. Waited. The shriek dying to a moan. Then silence again.

Menula closed the door behind him and went off down the corridor with his usual purposeful stride—neither fast nor slow. The walls seemed to tremble with the silence that hung behind him.

In the room, the old man lay in his bed, his arm hanging over the edge. His mouth hung open and his eyes gaped to the ceiling. Taula stepped out from behind the curtain where he had hidden. He went and leant over the old man, staring into the distorted face, reading the terror of death upon it frozen into the very flesh which was already growing cold. Tears poured down his cheeks as he closed the old man's haunted eyes.

That done, he sat on the edge of the bed, feeling that tormented spirit still in the room. His own doubts tore at him. The old man had entered mystery now beyond the reach of any knowledge which he had. And yet, had entered those shadows with such fear. And for himself? Could he have faced them either? He shook his head, then suddenly became aware of the danger should he be found in this room with a murdered man. If he were to accuse Menula, no one would stand with him. No one. And with so little achieved, he could not afford to be named for such a deed himself.

Cautiously he opened the door and peered out to see if anyone was around. No one was. He made his escape speedily, unobserved. In his own small cell, he sat hunched on his plank bed, his head abuzz with thoughts. It seemed that suddenly his appointed task was snatched out of his hands, leaving him bewildered. If it was not that, what was he meant to do? Suddenly he knew nothing. Nothing, nothing, nothing. He beat his fist against the wood, tortured by uncertainty.

'Sir?'

It was one of the boy messengers, He must have already knocked without being heard and opened the door, thinking the occupant to be asleep. He looked up at him questioningly.

'Sir, I am bidden to bring you to our Lord,' whispered the boy.

Taula stood in the secret chamber, stunned by what he saw there. Before him, suspended by a golden chain, was a transparent globe and from it echoed the tremors of some terrible power. Though no sound came from it, yet he seemed to feel a trembling in the air, as if it was pulsating deep within his own body. Responding to its inner intensity, he approached it, unaware of anyone else who might be in the room. The wonder lay within this globe. It was glowing with some inner power that gave it a certain translucency. He gazed at it.

The surface seemed to shift and blur as he looked at it. The impression it gave was of seas and land masses, mountains and rivers, but all was in movement. He went nearer and each place he looked at came clearly to his eyes as if he had turned a magnifying glass upon it. As he looked away, it faded and some other place came clear. A magical vision brought clarity wherever he set eyes. On the lands were mountains, hills and valleys. Rivers divided them. A sky hung over it all. People, tiny and distant, stood within the villages and lay down within the houses of the villages. Dogs lay before fires within the houses.

All was totally still. The True Lord watched him closely but he stood back in shadow where Taula could not see him.

'What a magnificent thing it is!' breathed Taula.

'This is the world itself that we are living on. On that sphere is every creature now living on this world of ours. Within those seas live the great white fish. In the trees are even the birds. See!'

He led Taula round to the other side of the globe and there, suspended by some mysterious means, was the Sky Fleet.

'But what is it for?'

'You will see. Wait! Any moment now and you will see everything.'

They waited and Taula walked round and round the marvellously detailed model, constantly exclaiming upon some new discovery. There came a knock on the door of the secret chamber. Hastily the True Lord of Atlantis opened the door and admitted Menula, who bore in his hands a steaming bowl. He carried it over to the globe and carefully the True Lord took it from him. Menula left the room with scarcely a glance towards the wonder that dominated the room.

'Take the bowl for me.'

Taula held it with shaking hands. Seeing only by the dim glow from the heart of that globe, the bowl looked full of some dark liquid. It felt warm to his hands. The True Lord took it from him.

He moved closer to the globe. There was an opening in the top of the transparent globe and there must have been liquid within it. He poured the contents of the bowl into the hole and the clear liquid turned colour as it swirled down through the hole.

Taula almost choked with disgust. The freshly added liquid was blood. Fresh blood. And a moment further on he knew whose blood it was. As the blood red liquid now obscured the whole surface of the globe, his mouth tightened.

'It had to be a Master's blood' said the True Lord. 'With no heart, I cannot give a soul to this world of mine.'

Taula grew calm. In truth, he was fascinated by the change going on within that transparent bowl. Gradually now, the red liquid was clearing, becoming transparent again. They could see the world easily again, but now it was in motion. The sense of its power now filled the room.

'It's turning!'

'More—look closer.'

And the people moved, the dogs scratched, the seas tugged at the land. The whole world was animated, each portion coming clear and fading as his eyes searched the globe.

'I don't understand this!' he whispered with holy dread.

'This is the Simulator—the world in miniature. Everything that happens in the real world happens here also. And one day what happens here will affect what happens in the real world.'

'You have made life.'

'We have copied life. There's still a difference.'

They both watched the globe, now in scarcely perceptible motion.

'How was this done?'

'Through the work of centuries. First we had to break life down, to take its secrets from it. Then we had to build it up again, experimenting time and time again until we managed to capture the essence of it—the heart which lives.'

'This is what we have worked for!' breathed Taula.

'And it can all be yours as well! Yours and mine both, my brother.'

Taula looked into his eyes, the first time he had ever really stared at the True Lord of Atlantis. He recoiled as he saw what he saw.

'No!'

They looked at each other, mirror twins, Taula stared into that face which so exactly matched his own.

He reeled back with the shock, holding his hand before his face. 'No, no, no!' he cried and shook his head, trying to drive the knowledge from his mind, but 'yes, yes, yes' surged deep within him and this truth terrified him more than all the rest. A stirring into life of the seed which destiny had planted—the power to move the world, the strength to turn all men to his ways, the destiny for which he had struggled. He had a vision, as though down through a long deep tunnel of all the centuries of struggle, loss and power, a great cry from a thousand voices all of whom had known him, known them, and would know them both again, the sudden coming together of his lifetime's study into this rising tide which could not be turned until his fate was played out fully—power. And that other side, that poor boy brought into the temple and beaten for his little sins, trembled deep within and almost died. Staggering under the buffeting storm, watched by that other brother, suddenly something sweeter stronger purer reached out into his swirling darkness and cut through it like a crystal knife and peace came to him. The surge came under his control, not spilling over him now but held within him, ready for whatever use he might have for it. His weapon—secrecy of mind, safe even from this long-matched brother—guarded the light from any other's eyes and kept it burning deep inside his heart.

'Born matched together since the beginning of time, my brother in spirit.'

'No!' he said, playing the part now of a soul still lost and staggering, not daring to show that there was light inside him.

'Why do you think you were brought here? How else would you have been admitted unless it was the weight of destiny which impelled it?'

'But—' he shook his head as if unable to face the barrage of revelation.

'This world which I have made, using your own Master's blood, this world is to be shared by two of us. Thus, one shall guard while the other sleeps and so on round. Only in this way shall we truly control the destiny of the greater world, through this our smaller world.'

'Why me? Why?' he cried, sounding as though his mind still whirled, as if all his reason had in a moment been reduced to a rubble of madness.

'We are brothers from all time before, twin souls locked on one path. You are needed here by me.'

'—I need to think—to have time—I can't—' Taula could not seem to find the words. It was as if he was fighting to hold back everything which threatened to well up from deep within and, whatever happened, that could not be allowed.

'Go into the shrine and give yourself time. There is still enough space between ourselves and action, we cannot gain control over the greater world without the jewel from the Heart of the Ice and, for that, we must wait until the Fleet return. As they will do!'

Taula staggered from the room, reeling under the discovery. But, instead of going to his own little cell or even to the inner shrine as he had been instructed, he went out of the building altogether and made his way full speed into the city, not stopping to check the safety of what he did. And, as he went, Menula— with his nose for danger—followed him.

They gathered all about him, trying gently to soothe him.

'You told me nothing!' he accused them. 'You deceived me. All of you deceived me!'

'It was not time,' said the blind astrologer. 'It would not have been right to tell you before!'

'But what is the connection between us?' cried Taula.

'What did he tell you?'

'That we were brothers of old, of time long before.'

'It's true. We have struggled from the first days of the world and many times came near to victory, but never as near as this.'

'How did it start?'

The blind astrologer came forward. 'The beginning isn't clear to us now. We knew once, but our knowledge has grown less perfect. We believe that you and he were twins born of a woman who mated with a sorcerer. He brought darkness into the world for the first time—before him there was only daylight—and in that darkness the brothers killed their mother. We don't know why, or even which brother did the act. But they were cursed, the pair of them, and ever since have tried to win the power of darkness for themselves, while we have tried to win the power of light.'

'But why am I with light? It seems to me it wasn't always so.'

'It's true. Our knowledge isn't full enough to know. It seems there was a woman but more we cannot tell. But we knew if you could be brought up only knowing light, then you would help us overthrow him—in this life or another.'

Taula took out the pure gold dagger which they had given him.

'I thought it was for the old man. I went in there prepared to kill him—'

'We couldn't tell you until the truth itself was revealed. Now you know what must be done. It is to kill the True Lord of Atlantis that you have been trained by us all these years.'

'But what will happen?'

'We shall be ready for the rest of them, the Templars.'

'I feel as if I must be going mad. So many things are tearing at my mind—so many! And he—he seems like some part of myself. If I kill him, do I kill myself?'

'Be courageous—for a little while more. We've all waited so long. We'll be with you. Wait for our signal and—'

'Wait!' said the watchman and hushed them into silence. They all listened and could hear the inexorable rap of footsteps coming towards them. They stared at the doorway, hypnotised.

'It's Menula,' whispered one as the door crashed inwards. He stood outlined hugely in the doorway, blinking as the candlelight drove darkness from his eyes.

'Well, clerkling,' he sneered. 'So tell me why you come creeping to this company of old men and young fools?'

They were fascinated by him. He stepped in among them, his massive paw already on his sword. Taula's one good hand tightened on his golden dagger but the blind astrologer sensed his movement and laid his hand on Taula's warningly.

'Let our young men take him,' he murmered. 'The dagger is for one heart only.'

Three young men edged forward and suddenly rushed Menula. Dragging his sword from the sheath, he swung wildly at them. Cowardice was not one of his faults and, although he stood no chance against the pack of them, he sliced bravely about him.

It was a brief and bloody encounter and they brought him to his knees in his own blood on the altar floor. They struck him again and again with their blades and still he struggled, his lips curled back in a snarl. One of them took a stick and beat him across the head with it and with a sudden dying surge of strength he righted himself and pushing them aside, went for the door. Although they followed him immediately, the movement took them by surprise. They followed his trail of blood right to the edge of the river and searched everywhere for him, then returned and reported that he must have drowned down in those chilly waters. Only Taula had the feeling that they might be wrong. They stood there panting.

'Get back before anyone else can see you aren't there. Wait for our signal.'

He stumbled from the bloody encounter, mumbling to himself, and they looked at each other.

'If he should fail us now—'

'He won't. He's the one who will save us all—'

'Unless we have been wrong about him.'

'No doubts now! We can't afford them.'

'It will all be well,' said the blind astrologer. 'It will be well.'

16

I<small>T</small> was a continent of ice. Plains, mountains and frozen rivers. Caves and valleys carved out by winds and time in gleaming bluegreen ice. It was a land that knew no winter, for there was only one season there—the season of ice. The sun flashed back at them from every facet and angle until they were all half-blind.

Even in this wilderness of cold there was life. Great furry bears lumbered across the snow, pausing here and there to scoop fish out of holes in the ice. Birds preened their oily feathers, darting swift glances towards the new arrivals out of tiny bright eyes. There was no alarm from them, for these invaders were no enemy that they recognised.

They stood unsteadily on the ice, more used to the steady pitch and toss of the sky-ships. The ice beneath their feet was flashed with running scars where the ballast log had struck it as they anchored. Their breath spiralled up all about them. Above them, the fleet was tethered together.

The captains all stood together around Arguilo and Bron. Aramin reached inside his coat and produced a package which he then proceeded to unwrap. They all watched. Inside the wrapping was a map, a very old one on which almost all the lettering was worn away. It was made of soft hide.

'How old is this?' asked Arguilo.

'When the Templars first came to Atlantis this map was already old.'

Arguilo looked from Bron to Aramin and suddenly noticed that each wore an identical jewel at his throat, a tiny diamond on a gold chain. Something began to buzz in his head. A recognition.

'What is this—a conspiracy?'

'No, a plan laid centuries ago. Not by us.'

'By whom?'

'By those who would save Atlantis from the Templars.'

'I don't really understand this,' said Arguilo in confusion.

'You mean there was a time when there were no Templars? Is that what you're saying?'

'Atlantis has risen and fallen before this. A great deal of evil has already gone into the Darkworld from Atlantis. Our people have tried to prevent that happening again. It lies in our hands. Ours—and yours, if you will trust us.'

'I'll trust you,' he sighed.

Aramin showed him the map. 'Here, where we've anchored, is the site of the hiding place. Now, before we can go to the Jewel, it's essential that we undertake a Cleansing Ritual. No man may approach the Jewel with evil in him. If he does, he may be destroyed. If you will allow it, I shall hold the ceremony and give my protection to your captains.'

'I permit it.'

'Speak with them first. They must be willing to follow me. You'll have to make them trust me.'

Obediently, almost without any will of his own, Arguilo did as Aramin asked him to do. Aramin and Bron waited while Arguilo went and spoke seriously with the captains.

'I can hardly believe that we, of all generations, will be allowed to see the Jewel,' murmured Aramin.

'It was written,' Bron answered in a matter of fact tone, but even he was moved. 'Do they not know what it will do?'

'The Templars? They only know of its magical powers. No one outside the White Company knows that it is the secret heart of Atlantis. No one, except our company, knows that it was taken to a place of safety so long ago. That is our knowledge alone.'

Aramin glanced up at the sky. There was some darkening in it, or perhaps in his eyes as he looked up into the sky. Whatever the cause, he felt uneasy. He knew that there was little enough time for delay.

'Come, either obey me and trust me, or go without the Jewel, for you will never find it for yourselves.'

They made haste to do as he told them. He intended to create a ritual of power, to draw out the answering power of the Jewel in the Heart of the Ice. There was no other way to uncover it, hidden as it was somewhere—anywhere—in this protected plain of ice and snow. He instructed them in the chant of protection, making them form a holding circle. In this he could conduct the ceremony in safety without being open to attacking powers while his own power was held inside the ritual. They followed the chant he gave them easily and felt themselves being drawn away into some region outside yet deep inside themselves. Aware of their bodies—the hair prickling on their arms and necks, an inner trembling—and yet divorced from them as if their minds were elsewhere, under some different control. As they gradually sank away from themselves, unable to do more than obey, a mist grew up around them and closed them together even more and cast their minds even further out of their own control. They were sweating against the feel of the icy mist. Their muscles strained, the very fibre of their bodies seemed to shriek against the effort demanded of them. The words of the chant slipped away from their minds. It seemed—they knew it was not so—that creatures were writhing out of the mist towards them.

Aramin could feel the creatures too, but he was not disturbed by them. He could say nothing for he was concentrating too hard upon the ritual itself, but the creatures were only given birth by the tremendous energy raised by the ceremony. They had no real existence and could not break the circle. They could only sniff helplessly at its edge, like stray dogs drawn by a kitchen. He took them through the whole ritual which was to call out the essence of the Jewel in order that it might reveal itself to them.

How much time went by and how many creatures crawled outside the circle of iron flesh, afterwards they could not recall. They held against the whole confusion of force and sound.

Aramin raised his hands to stop them. The chant faded. The mist cleared as suddenly as if someone had rolled it away from them. The day opened up again. They relaxed.

'Now,' said Aramin, 'we follow the map.'

He led them through the lanes of ice, between white walls that arched and twisted on each side of them. They were silent, awed by their surroundings. Their footsteps crackled over the surface of the frozen land. A lone seabird called mockingly and its voice echoed in the emptiness.

He paused by an opening in the face of ice. 'Did you bring lights?' he asked.

Balio produced the flare and flint. Aramin took them and struck a spark against the oil-soaked flare. It threw up black smoke then settled to a steady flame.

'Are we going in there?' asked one of the captains, with some apprehension in his voice.

'Yes,' said Aramin, 'and before we do, I want to say something. This journey won't be easy. The map we have is clear but what we don't know is what will happen as we follow it. No matter what you see and hear, you must keep together. Remember that none of the creatures you may see or hear can touch you or hurt you unless you break from the company. And when we come near the Jewel, you must keep your eyes turned from it. You must not touch it until I have wrapped it in the sacred cloth I have with me. If you do, it will destroy you.'

Aramin stepped into the opening and one by one they went in

after him, Bron bringing up the rear. They looked about them uneasily. The walls of the tunnel were dark but when the flare lit on them, they could see that they were solid ice. The coldness struck at them and they shivered and then grew too cold to shiver any more.

Arguilo was surprised that the air remained pure, even though they were obviously going down into the depths of the ice. But there was much that was strange about this place. Something was living there, for they heard its noise, somewhere in the shadows about them. When they wanted to halt, Aramin commanded them sharply onwards. Several of them felt something cold brushing their faces but when the light fell on the walls beside them, there was only the ice shining.

'There are others here,' muttered one of them.

'Don't fear them. They have always dwelt here alone,' Aramin told them.

There was a shout of laughter at his words, but it did not come from any of the captains of Atlantis. They moved together now, fearing that they might be snatched away from each other in the darkness.

The air grew thicker and warmer. They could feel the place pressing down on them.

'Use these words,' Aramin instructed them, and gave them the secret words. 'Repeat them silently throughout the journey. Think only of them and of following each other. Let nothing else come into your thoughts.'

Arguilo felt uneasy. The tunnel had closed about them and he could scarcely breathe. But he followed Aramin's orders and repeated the words. Whether or not it was his imagination, he felt as if his lungs were clearing a little. As it grew warmer, the walls ran with water and the floor was slippery with it. From time to time they stumbled and each time it happened Aramin warned them to repeat the formula of protection. They had the sense of others following close behind them but Aramin warned them not to look back. Bron could feel something shuffling at his ankles but when he tried to see what it was the shadows seemed to gather thickly round them. Sometimes one of the men would feel a blow which was strong enough to throw him against the running wet walls but when he put out his hand to fend them off only his companions were near.

Great though the heat grew it was not enough to melt the heart of this passage of ice. The air was more foetid now. In the distance they could dimly see a reddish glow and they headed towards it eagerly, like moths to a flame. When they came nearer to it, they stopped—shocked by what they saw. There, somehow burning within the ice itself, were flames on either side of the passageway.

'Pass between them. Don't be afraid. They're guardian lights, set there to keep safe the secrets of the ice,' Aramin called and as they passed between them the lights flared more brightly and lit their way more thoroughly. The tunnel seemed to dip down more sharply now. They were having difficulty in keeping their footing, but they struggled down into the heart of the ice.

'Take out your swords,' he told them. 'We will need them now we are near the Jewel. We will draw all evil creatures to us to their destruction as moths burn themselves on flames, whether they would or no.'

So it proved. The creatures that lived there in the darkness came to them. They could feel them brushing past their feet, tugging at their arms. Some of them could even feel sharp little teeth viciously biting into their flesh. The flare was extinguished by an evil wind and they had to go through darkness. Aramin held ready the cloth of silk.

They cut out into the darkness, hampered by the need to beware of each other. Bedlam broke loose about them as they struggled down the tunnel. The creatures of the ice were crowding about them, screaming abuse in languages never heard since life was first made. Primaeval curses and the basic evil which breathed in the mud of the Darkworld and fed on the twisted desires of men. It could have driven a man mad whose heart was not set on the Jewel, but they were as sure of themselves as the moon on its course. So they sliced through the bodies which barred their way to the heart of the sanctuary and when they finally gained access they were able to see, in the glow which Aramin knew was the warmth from the jewel, how successful their fight had been.

They cried out as they looked at each other. They were covered in blood and dark stains, as if vile substances had oozed all over them. Their swords were smeared with it and some of the metal looked scorched. The men were covered with ragged scratches and torn skin, as if claws had raked them, and they shivered with the disgust of it all.

'Come, we are almost there,' said Aramin encouragingly and they could in fact feel the truth of what he said. All the vile things that had pestered them had fallen away, creeping back into the lost depths from which they came. Now no creatures of darkness tugged and chewed at them, no evil waking dreams brought visions to them. They were free of all tainted beings. But more, they could feel that they were approaching something more powerful than anything they had dreamed of, something which was now pulling at them and yet disturbing them deep beneath their hearts and minds. They were profoundly uneasy, yet excited.

'We are very near,' said Aramin in a strained voice. 'Don't be afraid. Don't let its power shake you.'

The tunnel glowed deep red, becoming brighter and clearer and they plunged down into the lowest point. Then suddenly the way ahead twisted and as they rounded the sharp blind bend they all gasped. They found themselves in a cavern as brightly lit as day, burning as if a naked sun were suspended there. Several of them covered their eyes and the others did so when Aramin spoke.

'Cover your faces,' he said sharply. 'Cover them!'

They did so, but the light still seemed to burn right through the bones of their hands.

'Don't uncover them until I have wrapped the Jewel.'

He took out the cloth of silk and approached the source of light. He was murmuring the secret words of protection but he was terribly aware that they were perhaps not strong enough. He could feel its power battering at his mind and his concentration was wavering. If it fell ...

He was face to face with it now and it was brighter, stronger, than he had ever imagined. It blazed more than diamonds, with a dreadful life of its own, life enough to crush his own and disperse its scattered fragments in darkness. Nevertheless, he reached out, seized it from its niche of ice and cast the silk tightly around it. Abruptly the light faded, for the silk had been prepared for a thousand years already and had a power to curb the Jewel of its most destructive light.

'Now,' he said, 'we have the Jewel!'

They traced their footsteps back up through the ice. The tunnels and the caves were silent, emptied of all life and spirits. Still with swords drawn, unable to believe that the worst was really over, they walked cautiously, following Aramin who was enveloped in the dim glow of the Jewel.

He could feel the burden painfully. Not the heat exactly, not the light precisely, and yet some dual burden of the two. But it was not the physical weight, it was some terrible nearness that the Jewel had to the inside of his own mind which he could not understand, nor prevent. He searched for the words of protection which they had given him but they slipped somewhere just outside his memory and he could not call them back again. Still, he had the Jewel. He had the Jewel or ... did the Jewel have him? Have his mind? Did ...? Was ...? He shook his head. With all that light inside his brain, it was very difficult to think what he had been thinking just a moment before. In fact he could not ... could not ...

'Aramin!' Bron called warningly as Aramin staggered. Bron had some idea of what was happening to Aramin but even he did not realise how bad it was. He hurried forward to stop Aramin's fall but as he caught hold of his arm Aramin spun round, his eyes blazing.

'Don't think I don't know what you're doing!' Aramin hissed.

'It's all right,' Bron soothed him but Aramin was not in the state to be reached by that.

'Take your hand off me,' snarled Aramin. 'I know what you want, but you won't get the Jewel.'

'Come on,' said Bron insistently.

Aramin stumbled on, muttering angrily to himself though he was hardly aware of what he was doing or saying. He knew reality was slipping away, to be hidden in a blaze of burning light. The light which he felt as an acid pain in his heart, cauterising any darkness which had been within.

It seemed to take longer to get out than it had to reach the depths. Perhaps it was the almost-silence which did it. The clump of heavy shoes on ice, the drip of water in the shadows, the breathing, the murmuring from Aramin. They were glad to reach daylight at last. They stood about, dazed in sunlight, their eyes stinging with water. Arguilo gazed up at the Sky Fleet hovering above, then Bron touched his arm and called him aside to where Aramin was standing, still clutching his terrible and precious prize to him. Tears were streaming from his eyes, but not for light or sun.

'Aramin,' said Arguilo gently, but Aramin seemed not to hear him but stood with those passionless tears flowing from dead eyes. Bron sighed and put his arm about the Technician's shoulders. 'Come,' he said tenderly, 'bring your burden to its home,' and he slowly led Aramin up the ladder to the master ship. The other captains did not realise there was anything badly wrong, apart from the weariness of their long and frightening journey.

Arguilo followed, knowing that Aramin had been destroyed

by the power of the Jewel.

That evening, an important feast was held and the ships were hung with lights until the night sky blazed. The members of each craft wandered from one ship to another, renewing old friendships and making fresh ones. Normally, they each lived as if in a tiny village but on feast days they mixed freely together.

Larn came back to the master ship for the evening and Pala greeted him gladly but with a certain reserve. So much had happened since they had last been together under happy influences that she almost felt that it was not she who knew him. It had been some other Pala who barely remembered this wide-mouthed boy.

'Hallo!' he grinned, but there was an awkwardness in him too.

She smiled, glanced up and saw Bron watching them shrewdly. She blushed and Larn caught his eyes too. He looked from Pala to Bron, questioning and then shrugged and laughed.

'Am I not to be spoken to?' he asked.

'Of course,' she said in surprise and the barrier was eased between them.

In fact, it turned out to be an evening of extraordinary gaiety. Pala gradually found that it was no longer hurtful for her to see Larn. He had grown up during his secondment to Balio's craft and now he treated her with more concern and without the heavy dependence that had first drawn them together. For her part, she was no longer so worried about his good opinion and this adjustment between them made them better friends than before.

Arguilo was lighthearted. He and the twins' mother went from one group to another, pausing to gossip and enjoy themselves with everyone. The men drank well and the wine made them loud in their pleasure. It was an evening they remembered later.

The voyage back had to be routed around the long coast which lay between the fleet and Atlantis. There was no point in risking a return through the Forbidden Country. It was obvious that the Templars had made contact there. The dangers would be too great.

The next event was also inevitable. That they would meet the other part of their own fleet. Arguilo knew it. All of them knew it. And so it happened.

'There they are!' said Bron grimly.

Kerin screwed up his eyes against the sun. Through the brightness he could see the silhouette of the ships. Targon called the sailors ready to take up weapons and the fleet drew together, slowing their rapid flight almost to a standstill. The oncoming fleet did likewise, and they met almost stationary. Marrad appeared at the deck rail.

'Come on board,' called Arguilo and, to his surprise, Marrad agreed.

'Watch for treachery,' Bron warned him.

'Don't worry.'

Marrad came aboard. He climbed very slowly, painfully, seeming to find it hard to get his footing and having to be helped by a sailor. Several times he could not grasp a rope and had to pause and try again. Bron watched, his mind searching back to something familiar about this slightly spastic movement. As Arguilo spoke, Bron recalled where he had seen it before. Many years ago, Marrad's father moved like this. He had ended his days lying helpless in the sunlight, rolling one finger against another as if he was making pellets of bread, his palsied head nodding involuntarily.

Arguilo greeted Marrad politely but coldly. Marrad bowed his head. He looked ill, now that they saw him close to. His face was gaunt and his head and hands shook with fine tremors.

'Are you returning from the Ice Lands?' he asked Arguilo wearily.

'We are.'

'With the Jewel?'

'Yes.'

Marrad nodded again. He looked tired, as if an aeon of sleep would not assuage his weariness.

'How is it with you?' asked Bron and Marrad knew his condition had been recognised. He smiled sadly.

'As you see.'

'What's wrong?' persisted Arguilo. 'Are you sick?'

'You know already, don't you?' he said at last. It's the same illness that took my father and his father too, and now it has come to me.'

There was little to be said. He spoke the truth and they could see the mark of the illness on him.

'And the fleet?' asked Arguilo.

Marrad shrugged.

'Why should I lie?' he said. 'I have nothing to win now. They see the illness on me too. Some of them say it's a judgment on me. Others, that the Templars are destroying me. Whatever, they don't want to follow me further.'

'You mean they want to unite the fleet again?' said Bron incredulously.

'What else can they do? They're afraid.'

The talk went on, but the main part was said. Without struggle and without argument, the fleet was coming together again, all because Marrad was stricken by the illness of his line.

The fleet travelled together and when they stopped that night they harnessed the whole fleet together. Arguilo slept easily. He was glad enough to welcome his own back again. He wanted no revenge on them. It was enough that they had come back into the circle again.

17

I⊤ was night and Taula still paced about his room. He was tired but too restless in hi mind to be able to sleep. He lived always on guard now and had not seen the True Lord since awakening to the truth of his identity.

Since he had known, the power had grown in him. He could feel it as an energy which he could scarcely control sometimes and all those around him felt it too. They treated him with a respect which had never been there in their dealings with him before. The servants cringed before him although he did not change much in his manner to them. But the feeling was there. The power had come, and they knew it and feared it.

The priests were preparing him for his position and he spent the days in study with them. The nights were spent partly in meditation and partly simply trying to contain the growth of his strength.

*   *   *

They were coming towards land and their hearts were filled with all kinds of doubts. Since they could only have asked each other questions to which they did not know—or dreaded—the answers, they kept instead a silence which was louder than any argument. The entry into Atlantis was much upon their minds. The captains attended to their duties but with abstracted minds. Arguilo kept staring into the distant horizon as though he would pull the future out of it with will-power alone and devour it like a poison-taster for them all. Bron hung about him, half-casual, and Arguilo fed upon the comfort of his presence. The future was almost ready to break upon them and whether it would bring darkness and terror, or triumph and light—who could know and who dared to wonder?

The doubt moved like infection through them all. Even the humblest ones among them, having no idea of what was taking place, felt something. The sailors were uneasy. The women strangely silent. Even the children seemed subdued. By the time they came towards the misty green lands of Atlantis, a sense of doom was widely spread among them all.

As they approached near enough to distinguish the little fishing boats bobbing in the bay, the captains were standing on the decks. The craft came gently to rest high above the harbour and Arguilo leaned over the edge to peer more closely at what he seemed to see below.

'Ay, they're waiting for us,' Bron grunted.

The harbour wall was black with figures.

'Should we wait up here for them to come to us?' murmured Arguilo.

Bron considered this for a moment, then shook his head.

'It wouldn't be a good idea, to assert our territory now. They could drag us down right out of the skies if they wished. Let us show willingness to co-operate, while we've got the advantages.'

The ladders were lowered to the harbour wall and Arguilo made his way down to the quay, watched by Bron.

'Arguilo the Fleet-Master?' asked a tall pale man who stepped forward. His eyes were cold, his lips thin, and he had a drawn sword in his hand. Two men came with him.

'Yes?' said Arguilo.

'Excuse me, Lord, but I have orders to take you chained to the palace of the Templars and all your captains too.'

He signalled and the men came forward, chains wrapped around their thick arms. They swiftly bound him in chains, almost before he had time to absorb what had happened.

'Please order your captains down here,' said the cold-eyed officer.

'I ... I ...' Arguilo was stunned.

'Lord, it would be best,' he urged, 'otherwise I have orders to take the children.'

By now Bron had come swiftly down the ladder and was standing before them both.

'I'll bring the captains down,' he said quietly and went up to relay the message to them all. As stunned as Arguilo, they came forward and stood on the decks with Bron. Children peered out of the doorways with frightened eyes, their mothers holding them tightly. The sailors stood round them, just as helpless.

'What are we to do?' asked a rough old bosun.

'Wait here for our return,' said Bron, 'and take care of our people until then.'

'Do you think you will return?' asked the bosun very quietly to Bron. 'Have we lost everything after all?'

'Have some courage, man,' Bron urged. 'Remember our promises—and our strength, and have trust in the light that has never failed us yet.'

He started to climb back down the ladder, followed by the captains one by one. The women, the children, the sailors crowded to the edges of the decks to watch them and said nothing to each other as their captains far below were put in chains and tied together like a train pack of animals. Ahead of them all strode Arguilo and Bron, Bron still striding as though he were free and proudly so. The bosun smiled to himself and felt a surge of hope there in his heart—a feeling not shared at that moment by any other member of the Sky Fleet.

Arguilo saw nothing of the dark streets and alleys through which they were led. He tasted bile in his mouth and fear in his belly. The chafing of the irons on him were nothing beside the burning despair inside his heart. It was taking all his self-control to fight the weakness of his bowels at that moment.

'Remember the white fish,' whispered a voice in his ear. Bron. And suddenly an image of that majestic beast carving his way through the great sea came to him and something untied within him for a moment. Keeping that symbol, that great conqueror of the oceans, within his heart kept terror at bay. All this—the chains, the indignities—were not more than storms and breaking waves. He was determined that he would lead the sky-people free again. He straightened consciously and took on a prouder step.

Pale Atlanteans stood in doorways to watch them go by. Their eyes told nothing, their faces even less. They stood and stared expressionlessly at these big bronzed men marching by all clad in chains. They were smaller by far, these land people, more slim and somehow with less life in them. Unless that was the effect of their pallid skins and their unsmiling faces.

The city swallowed them into its embrace of stone. The alleys which threaded through it were dark and damp. High above the houses leaning in to each other a patch of sky peered down at them, as far off as a farewell. The streets, when they were not just mud, were cobbled and the captains kept stumbling, unused as they were to still ground.

To men who had spent their life above the ocean the stench of the city was overwhelming. They could see into some of the houses as they passed and what they saw made them shudder. Dim courtyards, tiny windows, decaying walls and windows with faces peeping whitely out. Crumbling statues of strange gods

138

stared malevolently at them out of dingy shrines. Old women at the wells turned suspicious eyes upon them.

They were trapped. Not only by chains. But also by the streets among whom they were lost, by the walls, the very air of the city, by all that mass of staring strangers who followed them every step of their way.

As they approached the palace of the Templars, the streets widened and the dark huddle of scruffy houses fell back behind them. This was obviously the richer part of the city, yet not much more comforting. There was a bleakness about this wide boulevard which did nothing to reassure them. They were led across to the main entrance and taken inside the enormous building. They gaped about them, amazed that there could be walls so high. Corridors arched away into silence and indeed it was silence which spoke most loudly about this place. A silence, not of calm, but of nameless things working behind the cloak of soundlessness and they all felt it, even those who had never been singed by power before. Bron, recalling dimly the early years of his boyhood, found his hair prickling up and down his neck and his belly gripped with an ancient terror. But he was a man now, not a fearful boy, a man with power to call upon in turn and he refused to bow to the threat of any other force.

Through the corridors of stone, their leg chains dragging and clinking on the floor, their feet echoing, then swallowed by all that acreage of corridors again. Round corners into the same corridor, past the same windows, the same courtyards with the same fountains and the same secretive trees—or so it seemed. They were lost.

The captains were kept together in a cell with two surly guards to watch them, muttering to each other from time to time and staring insolently at the sky-people. Bron and Arguilo were taken away.

'The Master of the Templars,' said their escort, and bowed his way out of the room. At first sight, such a grand personage seemed to have an insignificant appearance. Pale too, and thin.

They stood there, uncertain of what to do. The Master of the Templars came over to them, saying nothing either. Coming closer. Bringing with him the reek of power so intense that it seemed to fill their nostrils, setting every nerve in their bodies jangling with anticipation. Bron looked into his face, searching those tired and all too knowledgeable eyes, and obviously finding what he was searching for, he suddenly knelt. Arguilo stood back, watching their interaction in fascination. He could feel the edge of what was happening. It bristled all along his spine, tugged at the rim of consciousness, but it was not clear. But Bron knelt there, bathed in the outpouring of light and power which came uncovered at last from Taula who had entered his spiritual kingdom.

Taula pulled him up.

'Brother,' he said and for the moment no more. Tears ran down his cheeks but he seemed unaware of them. After a short time more, he said: 'Come, we have no time to waste. Let us go to the Jewel. Where is it?'

'On our ship,' answered Arguilo.

'Then we must take it quickly. The moon reaches its height tonight and this is when we must strike him down, or he will strike us into darkness, and all will be to do again.'

He turned and flung out of the chamber, followed immediately by Arguilo and Bron. The guards fell back before him, for no one crossed the Master of the Templars, nor even would have thought of treason, lest his own thoughts be shadowed and he be marked down for death or something worse.

As they made their way through the streets again, still stumbling sometimes on the hard earth, Bron noticed that there was already a hint of evening in the sky and as he looked round further he saw a faint bright sphere which would be the moon in glory in a few hours time. It did not take long to get to the harbour. There were still a few of the black-clad guards on duty and they immediately sprang to attention as the Master of the Templars strode through them. He put Arguilo to wait below, with a guard to watch him for appearances sake, and he and Bron climbed the ladder. As they touched down on the deck, the sailors looked intently at Bron but he gave nothing away. At this stage, it was too soon. Instead he kept his eyes downcast, leading Taula into Arguilo's cabin. There, locked safely away in its wooden chest, was the Jewel. Taula, even with the urgency of the situation, paused, holding the Jewel in his hands. Eyes closed, feeling its power renewing him.

'Lord,' reminded Bron gently.

'Ah yes,' said Taula, rousing himself back into the urgent present again. Bron laid the Jewel back still wrapped in its cloth of white silk and closed the lid again. He tucked the chest under his arm and followed Taula.

'We must not let it out of our sight again,' said Taula, indicating the chest. Bron nodded.

They went down and walked back more slowly now, talking of what had to be done. The sun was sinking, bleeding across a watercolour sky, and the Atlanteans were hurrying for home. Atlantis was not a city where men would willingly walk out at night.

As they walked back through the lengthening shadows, a man stepped from a doorway, an old blind man.

'We are betrayed,' he cried, weeping as he spoke. 'I have been searching for you over all the city to warn you. Don't go back into the palace. He waits there for you.'

There was no doubt who 'he' was.

'Who betrayed us?' asked Taula, his voice quite calm.

'One of our own Company.'

'Where can we shelter now?' asked Bron urgently.

'Come with me,' said the old man and speedily tap-tapped his way through a city quickly darkening. He never faltered, his step made no less certain by the darkness which he could not see. He led them through a tangle of interlinked courtyards until they arrived in a dimly-lit place filled with the warmly sensuous smoke of incense.

'Here, you'll be safe here for a while,' said the old man, 'But he will soon break through the circle of protection we keep round here and the Jewel will draw him to you.'

'Ah, you know then?' said Taula.

'It drew me too. How else would I have found you?'

'What must we do?' Bron broke in.

'He will send his messengers after you,' said the old man. 'He must have that Jewel to finish off his work. Now he knows you have no intention of giving him the Jewel, he will have you first, then take the Jewel once you are dead.'

Bron shivered at the old man's calm recital but Taula was listening intently.

'Now he knows you will not join him, he must destroy you and this is how he will do it.' The old man bent closer to him, whispering into the silence while Taula heard him with the same concentration.

'I shall go now, before he knows for sure I have the Jewel on me.'

'I'll come too,' said Bron, but Taula restrained him. 'No, this is my battle now and you have no place in it. Stay here as you must, for the city is sealed now and he is with the Templars in the holy shrine, raising high magic's aid against me.'

'But what about you?'

'I have the Jewel. It is all I need.'

The old man blessed him and he slipped out into the darkness alone, the Jewel wrapped in silk and bound about his neck.

The streets were empty. It was a dark night, though it should not have been. No sounds disturbed the city which lay paralysed beneath the True Lord's seal.

'Where are the messengers?' Taula murmured aloud.

In answer a deep baying sound echoed about the houses and

the city trembled in fear. As he heard that noise, a vision came to him of deep caverns under the earth where no light or sound could come and only the naked bones of men huddled together for company. He was pale, but not yet afraid.

He squared his thin shoulders up and stepped firmly along the street meeting the evil bravely. It flowed round him and beyond him, its source the True Lord raising power in the Temple. The moon was still covered. He walked on, the pressure of that black power pushing against him like an invisible fog. He could hear that distant hound still baying, searching for him in the empty streets.

He was confident he could drive that creature of death away. Not for nothing had he spent his youth poring over those old formulas of protection and, with the Jewel too ... he shrugged.

The beast was coming nearer. A great coldness was growing around his heart, though he murmured the ritual words continuously. An uneasy streak of lightning darted across the dark sky and the clouds muttered with thunder. The moon was hidden. Suddenly as he entered a narrow street he found himself face to face with the beast. Huge and slavering, wild to get at him and have the prize—his heart. It dripped black saliva, red eyes shining, and made for him at a threatening lope, pausing suddenly as Taula threw a vicious ritual curse. It stopped and shook its head, bewildered and Taula tried to push the creature back out of the road. He could not. A small twinge of fear caught him then. He had to throw this creature out of the way, back to whatever stinking realm of hell that the True Lord drew him from. He knew he could destroy this thing, this filthy messenger of unclean death, so what was wrong? Why could he not break through its meagre power and cast it back into its own domain?

Only if the heart is pure, someone had told him once. Only if the heart is pure. So many years of darkness, so much misery, so many dead. The pure heart. If not pure, what then? He faltered and the beast drew nearer, so that he could smell its foetid breath.

It was then that he noticed the movement behind him. Half-turning, to watch on either side, he saw the figure approach, an old man bending over a staff, seeming to take what little strength he had from that sturdy rod. The hound came closer again, the old man drew nearer. His mind was whirling about, pulling back the formulas into his mouth, watching both ways, wondering, remembering—the pure heart ... the pure heart.

The old man was only feet away, covering the ground with painful slowness.

'Who are you?' cried Taula. The blind astrologer had talked only of the hound. The old man came nearer still until Taula stopped him with a seal of distance. The hound pressed closer, snarling.

'Tell me who you are?' said Taula.

The old man laughed with a high mad cackle.

'I am the end of all your hopes. I am the one who turns young beauties into decaying old women. I turn cities to dust and nations of men into dried bones.'

'Who?' muttered Taula, trying to keep the hound back too.

'I am Time,' whispered the old man triumphantly, drawing Taula down into his eyes of darkness.

He was almost lost in the deep of time, the pool of eternity in which all men died. He was falling into a space more deep and cold and heartless than any he had ever known, being torn away by time and crushed in those treacherous arms to become dust like the generations before him. The hound was baying louder.

'Come down, you powers of Malacheme,' he cried out desperately, 'and give to me your strength!'

The old man tottered back and his shape shifted and changed, allowing Taula to uncover him for a moment. The True Lord. As soon as he felt his disguise torn away by rough magic, the True Lord cursed him.

'What are you doing?' he snarled. 'I have offered you everything. Why are you trying to destroy my gifts to you?'

'I have my own path to follow.'

'We have our path together. You have no path of your own. That is a delusion fed to you by fools who would use you for their own ends. Do you really believe they're after good, you poor fool?' he jeered.

Taula muttered a spell and a thunderbolt crashed against a building above the True Lord's head. Stones scattered down all around him.

'Will you waste your strength in spells and sorcery like a witch?'

Taula aimed another at him and meanwhile moved in closer. The True Lord spoke to himself, no words aloud, and suddenly Taula felt something writhing over his feet. Glancing down he saw a great serpent arching about his legs. 'Back into the Depths of Hellemoth!' he ordered, shuddering with disgust as the vision shimmered into emptiness.

He tried to cast the hound back a little and to get nearer to the True Lord. He had to close right in on him, to be able to hold him. He searched his mind for a more powerful formula, and called on the Shades of Tabaroth to take the hound to themselves. The beast howled and then turned snarling towards the True Lord who tore his attention from Taula. He cursed the hound and sent it back into the dark regions. It was too dangerous to keep where Taula might be able to turn it against him, for such beasts will only serve who may be strongest. They have no other loyalty but that to power.

Taula leapt forward and grasped hold of the True Lord, trying to bind him with a spell. Suddenly he found he had a shapeless creature of a thousand arms and sinews clasped within the tight circle of his arms. A mass of struggling twisting stinking flesh, smooth and oily, sliding from his locked arms. He held fast, muttering spells of power to try to break the shape back into its human form. When it could not escape in that form, it changed again and became bright and burning so that great weals of fire came up on Taula's flesh wherever the two of them touched. Taula clenched his teeth and refused to release his prisoner. He cried tears of pain but did not heed them and he groaned with agony between the words of his spells, unaware that it was his own voice which uttered those groans.

Somewhere near he was dimly aware that noise and confusion were also walking the city streets, but he could not turn his attention there. He had to subdue the spirit of the True Lord. When the fire could not break him, the True Lord resumed his own shape and filled Taula's mind with horrors, one leaping fast after another. Rats and babies, snakes, blood and torment, confusion, images of terror, visions of disgust. Taula tried to cast them out of his mind or to ignore them but he was not as much master of the mind as the True Lord who had spent a lifetime mastering minds. He began to weaken and the True Lord mocked him triumphantly.

'Ah, so you thought you could challenge me! Don't you know your pride has betrayed you through the centuries, you poor idiot?'

But the White Company were gathering and coming to them. Through streets clothed by darkness and sealed by magic, they were approaching in answer to Taula's need of them. He knew they must be coming. He had to hold out for as long as he could, no matter if he went mad in doing so. He gathered strength to utter one more spell. As he did so, the True Lord momentarily let loose his hold and gave Taula the chance to grasp his wrist and plunge the golden dagger into his side. The True Lord cried out as the knife pierced his ribs. He reeled and went to his knees but he had lost none of his defiance. He threw a curse at Taula and scattered scorpions about his feet. Taula dodged them, his flesh crawling with horror.

'You can't kill me, you fool,' gasped the True Lord. 'It is written that I cannot be slain by human weapons.'

'But I can weaken you,' answered Taula panting. 'I have

stabbed you with a dagger of virtue and you will have no strength to use your magic on me.'

The True Lord stood up and stood swaying.

'We can't destroy each other, brother,' he said. 'We must keep together. We have no way of defeating each other.'

'That is no longer true,' said Taula in a strange voice, his hands busy. The True Lord looked up sharply and his eyes bored deep into his brother's.

'You have it, don't you?' he said almost gently.

Taula made no answer. He walked towards his brother, his face fixed rigidly. As he approached, the True Lord called down the creatures of the upper darkness to his aid and chaos and confusion stormed around them. Taula continued to walk, beyond heeding the tearing of the creatures about him. He faced his brother, their eyes locked and what they read in each other's eyes was unspeakable and unknowable. Taula unleashed the Jewel and held it high in his right hand. Then using the words that could be spoken only once in the history of the world, he thrust the naked Jewel into the True Lord's face. The True Lord threw up his hands and tried to find words to answer out of the dying wreck of his brain, but it was all burned away and he fell to the ground babbling like a crazed child, in a high-pitched keening voice. The beasts from darkness set on him and he had no way to turn them from him. They sent him in pieces and then turned their hungry jaws to Taula.

He was standing there, the Jewel dead in his grasp. Lifeless and fractured, with all its light discharged. Then the Jewel fell from his hand and as he looked down at his arm he saw and realised that it had withered and the flesh and muscles had all died too. He moaned and let himself fall, as if giving himself to those creatures of the night. With howls of triumph they leapt on him.

He found himself surrounded by the Company. Every one of them was clad in white, each bearing a golden sword as guardians against the spells of evil ones. An old man bent over him, the blind astrologer, wiping grime and blood from his cheek.

'He is awake,' announced the old man, feeling Taula's eyes upon him.

The members of the Company bent over him, murmuring blessings and prayers of thanks.

'The beasts?' he whispered.

'They're gone, Lord, back to their own places. We came just as you fell and we were able to cast them back.'

'And my brother?' he whispered.

'Lord, you have conquered,' Bron answered gravely. Taula felt no joy at this victory. Indeed, he seemed to feel nothing. Then Bron noticed his arm.

'Lord,' he started and Taula noticed his gaze.

'My own imperfections,' he murmured cryptically. 'But come, we have more to do yet before we finish this good night's work.'

They all set off together, the captains and the White Company, heading towards the Temple. The clouds were beginning to clear and the moon was flirting with the sky, seeming at every minute to be ready to give herself to the night.

'We must hurry,' said Taula more urgently. They quickened their pace.

They felt it when they were near, the waves of power, the echoes of something evil, the sense of darkness becoming tangible. The ceremony was coming to its height as they entered the shadows beside the Temple, Taula covering their way with a formula of secrecy. This was to have been the crowning ritual of the True Lord's secret intention. The start of the ceremony had called up the messengers of death and time: its finish would call up all the power of hell which he would take into himself and with the Jewel use the Simulator to give him power over all beings. To turn the Simulator from a model into a key to ultimate control.

Entered into the magical suspension of being, the Templars

knew nothing of the silent company which crept up to every entrance with their golden swords unsheathed. Nor of the captains who put the guards to heel through fear. Nor of their dead Lord, nor of the new one.

He swept up to the altar itself and struck the waiting chalice of blood to the ground. The Templars shuddered and woke from their trance. They stared up at this figure, standing before the very altar of hell. They watched, unmoving and unspeaking, as he called fully on the powers now at his command and split the altar before their eyes and cast it down in fragments. And when he ordered them to disperse, each to his own cell, to lock himself in and stay there until summoned, such was their terror that they obeyed him and left the sacred shrine broken to pieces and in his hands.

Leaving the noise and confusion behind him, Taula went to the Simulator and watched the little world turning. He should have been joyful but heaviness weighed inside him. He stood for a long time lost in thought.

'Lord, it is finished,' said Bron gently. 'Those who would not bow have bowed, and all the rest have died. Atlantis is yours.'

'And you, what do you want?' asked Taula.

'We want to serve Atlantis and be free to follow the great white fish.' They stared at the Simulator.

'And you,' said Bron. 'What do you want, Lord?'

But Taula made no answer.